To
Cara
Me

from
Mrs Ross

37

Make Me a Star

By the same author

Non-Fiction
Showing the Ridden Pony
Not Quite a Horsewoman

Fiction
I'd Rather Not Gallop
Caroline Canters Home
If I Could Ride
Eventer's Dream
A Hoof in the Door
Ticket to Ride
Flying Changes

CAROLINE AKRILL

Make Me a
Star

DRAGON
GRAFTON BOOKS
A Division of the Collins Publishing Group

LONDON GLASGOW
TORONTO SYDNEY AUCKLAND

For Em, and Sal and Glynne
To remind them of
their Drama School days

Dragon
Grafton Books
A Division of the Collins Publishing Group
8 Grafton Street, London W1X 3LA

Published by Dragon Books 1987

First published in hardback by
Grafton Books 1986

Copyright © Caroline Akrill 1986

ISBN 0-583-30972-0

Printed and bound in Great Britain by
Collins, Glasgow

Set in Times

All rights reserved. No part of this publication may
be reproduced, stored in a retrieval system, or
transmitted, in any form, or by any means, electronic,
mechanical, photocopying, recording or otherwise,
without the prior permission of the publishers.

This book is sold subject to the condition that it
shall not, by way of trade or otherwise, be lent,
re-sold, hired out or otherwise circulated
without the publisher's prior consent in any
form of binding or cover other than that in
which it is published and without a similar
condition including this condition being imposed
on the subsequent purchaser.

Contents

1

Not a Normal Part . . .

'Look, Moira,' the man with the clipboard was saying wearily as I pushed open the doors, 'we're looking for a teenager here, and I know for a fact that you're knocking thirty years old. I'm sorry love, but I really want a new face . . .' He passed a hand over his thinning hair and glanced unhappily at the dark-haired young man who was slumped in a chair by his side. By way of reply the young man pulled up the collar of his anorak and retreated into it like a hibernating tortoise. He closed his eyes.

The next girl stepped forward. She was pretty in an elfin way, dressed like a dancer, and could have been except that she was too skinny, lacking a dancer's muscle. Goose bumps pricked the thin nylon sleeves of her unitard. She gave the Casting Director a brilliant smile.

'Look, love,' he said with a sigh, 'can we take off those ridiculous shoes for a minute?'

The brilliant smile vanished. The elfin girl pushed up her leg-warmers and stepped reluctantly down from her five-inch glamour heels. Already her face had assumed an expression of defeat.

'You're just not tall enough, are you love? Five feet six minimum, we said. Yes, I know you can make the height with heels – I could make six feet myself with stilts, but we can't get away with anything less than the minimum this time, it isn't as if it's a normal part . . .'

I flopped into a vacant chair at the end of the line of waiting girls and I wondered if the word normal could be applied to anything at all in the world of stage and screen. I was feeling harassed and cross with Ziggy because the journey by tube and bus had been lengthy and expensive and tiresome, and now that I had arrived I could see that it had all been futile. There would be no work to be gained from this. I had been to more than thirty auditions since leaving theatre school, and I could recognize a doomed casting session when I saw one.

It was not that the church hall was anonymous and far-flung, with stone-cold antiquated radiators, orange plastic chairs and dusty floorboards, because that was typical enough; it had more to do with the stultifying blanket of gloom which hung over the proceedings. There was none of the nervous banter, the forced animation, the false gaiety of previous auditions I had attended. The air of palpable excitement, of tense yet hopeful anticipation was notably absent from this place. And there were other absentees. Three empty chairs, a scattering of paper cups and a circle of stamped-out cigarette ends behind the Casting Director told of interested parties who had long since lost hope and departed. The few remaining girls waited in glum silence. In an atmosphere such as this nobody could please, nobody could hope.

The elfin girl picked up her shoes and shuffled back to her chair to collect her coat. Without the glamour heels she was tiny, and looked about twelve years old. It was hard to understand why some people turned up to audition when they bore no resemblance to what was wanted. Not that I had the slightest idea what this particular Casting Director was looking for. Ziggy's last-minute telephone call had told me nothing apart from the fact that I should get myself out to the audition, pronto, within the hour, and 'play this one low key, Kiddo – nice jeans, a shirt, leave the hair loose, knot the jersey round the neck – got the gist, have you?' After which, before I could protest, question, he had rung off. I knew it was useless to attempt to ring him back. Messages for Ziggy reached him via The Café Marengo in Soho, a corner booth of which he utilised as his office when he was not hanging around the drama schools, the model agencies and the dance studios scouting for marketable, unsigned talent.

Ziggy was not a licensed agent, and what he did was probably illegal, but he always knew who was casting for what and where. He had taken me on when no agency would, and his percentage was ten per cent of my earnings instead of the usual fifteen – 'low overheads make economies possible, Kiddo.' Well, Ziggy, I reflected as I watched the last of the waiting girls present herself for inspection, you've got your money on a loser today.

Now it was my turn. The young man in the anorak did not even bother to open his eyes as I stepped forward. I was not sure what connection he had with the part on offer; for all I knew he could have been the producer, the director, the male lead, or the money, but I thought him bad mannered and I was annoyed. The Casting Director looked as though he could have used some support. Despite the fact that the hall was unheated and distinctly chilly he had been obliged to remove his jacket and roll up his shirt sleeves. Beads of desperation glistened on his brow. 'Cheer up a bit, love,' he pleaded. 'Smile a bit. Try to look pleasant. It's been a long day.'

'It's almost over,' I said. 'I'm the last. After me, you can *both* go to sleep.'

The dark-haired young man opened one eye. He frowned.

'Have you got a name?' the Casting Director said hastily.

'I'm Grace,' I said, 'Grace Darling.' I was not. My name was Grace Vincent. The Darling had been Ziggy's idea. 'You got to give them a handle they can latch on to, Kiddo, something that sticks in the old grey matter. Grace Darling's a peach.'

'Have you got an agent, Grace Darling?'

'Yes,' I said. 'Ziggy Stanislavski, Starlight Promotions.'

The Casting Director winced.

Unexpectedly the young man opened both eyes. 'Is that all your own hair,' he wanted to know, 'or are you wearing a piece?'

'I'm not wearing a piece.'

'Have you got Equity?' the Casting Director said.

'Now look here,' I said crossly, 'I thought you wanted a teenager, a new face? Because even with my limited experience I know that undiscovered teenagers don't usually have Equity membership.'

'All right, Grace Darling, keep your hair on.' The young man grinned.

I ignored him. The Casting Director said, 'What do you mean, with your limited experience? We're looking for a trained actress here, you know. We don't want any amateurs.'

'I'm not an amateur,' I said indignantly. 'I've done three years at stage school.'

'The Rose Jefferson, for a guess,' the young man put in. 'And I bet it cost Daddy a packet.'

I glared at him. This was a sensitive point. From my earliest schooldays I had wanted nothing but to become an actress. All my pocket money had been spent on theatre tickets and cinema seats, and when there was no money, I watched television. By watching others I had learned, and at Wallingford Grammar School I had been rewarded with the leading role in every dramatic production and my future had seemed assured. I had received much praise for my acting ability at school and I was confident that either The Royal Academy of Dramatic Art or the Central School of Speech and Drama would immediately recognize my talent and offer me a place. They did not. To my intense chagrin I failed both auditions twice.

After that I lowered my sights and auditioned anywhere and everywhere. The Rose Jefferson Academy had been the only school to offer me a place, and as it had not been accredited by the National Council for Drama Training, I had been unable to obtain a government grant. So yes, the Rose Jefferson had cost my father a packet, but it still did not mean that my acting diploma had been bought for me. I had worked extremely hard for it.

I decided it was pointless to continue and would have turned to leave, but the young man beat me to it. He stood up, stretched out his arms briefly as if to ascertain that they were still connected to his body, and with somewhat extravagant finality zipped up his anorak. 'OK, Melvyn,' he said, 'let's call it a wrap.'

The Casting Director stared at him. He looked distraught. 'You can't mean it,' he wailed. 'You can't mean that after all the hassle over the contract, after we've auditioned all these kids, you're backing out because you can't decide the female *lead*?' He pulled a handkerchief out of the pocket of his crumpled trousers and wiped his face with it, but really, I think he could have wept.

'We've got our female lead,' the young man said. 'I've just decided.'

The Casting Director's jaw dropped slightly. So did mine.

'I have just decided to take Grace Darling,' the young man said. 'Grace Darling will be our female lead. We will take Grace Darling, trained by the Rose Jefferson Academy, managed by Ziggy Stanislavski of Starlight Promotions, and we will make her into a star. Grace Darling will be perfect.' With sudden and surprising agility he capered away across the dusty floor, bowed in an exaggerated manner to the row of empty chairs, and finished up at the doors with a perfectly executed pirouette. As the doors swung back against his departure, an out-of-date calendar fell from the wall. Its pages fluttered in the silence like the wings of a wounded bird.

The Casting Director stared at me. I stared at the Casting Director. Neither of us could quite believe what we had heard. I didn't know what to think, but certainly I did not imagine that I had landed the part. Twenty auditions had shown me the competition. From twenty auditions I had learned that if one survived the first, there would be a second. After which there would be a short list. And after that, a short list compiled from the first short list. And even if one survived all that, until the very end, until the final three, the odds were still three to one against. And so I was not naïve enough to believe that I could simply walk into the tail end of an audition and be handed the female lead in whatever the production might be. And yet . . .

'I don't suppose he can actually *decide*,' I said. 'I don't suppose he actually has the *authority* . . .'

'You *bet* he has the authority,' the Casting Director told me. 'Don't you know Tom Sylvester? He's the writer of this little piece. If he doesn't get to chose the lead, we don't get the script. This contract's a killer.' He subsided into one of the hideous orange plastic chairs. The expression of incredulity on his face was unmistakably charged with relief. 'Oh glory,' he exclaimed, 'Oh, Jesus Christ, Superstar.'

I still could not believe it. It seemed the craziest way to land a part. 'But he can't have *meant* it,' I said. 'For one thing, he didn't even hear me read – he doesn't even know if I can act!'

'Now listen to me, Grace Darling,' the Casting Director said in a threatening voice, 'you had better be able to act. You had better be able to act because we've been holed up in this draughty barn of a place for two whole days; two hundred and twenty-seven females I've auditioned for this lead, and not one of them he's liked, not a flicker of the eyelid until you

13

came along, and normally I'd have short-listed a dozen by now. So let's forget he didn't hear you read, forget Rose Jefferson, forget Ziggy Stanislavski, because you've got yourself the part, Grace Darling, and you've got Equity as from this minute – you can ride?' he added.

Across the dusty floor and the stamped-out cigarette ends I looked at him in astonishment and disbelief. I felt stunned. It was utterly incredible and marvellous to think that I had a part, any part, and that I would be given my Equity card, the precious union membership that all actors and actresses need in order to work and which they cannot apply for until they are offered a part. I was not, however, prepared for the last question.

'Ride?' I said faintly.

'Ride,' the Casting Director said heavily. 'You've heard of horseback riding? It's supposed to be a sport – you wear a skid-lid to protect your brain, and you sit between the ears and the tail.' As the implication of my negative response hit him he stared at me, appalled. 'You must be able to *ride*, Grace Darling! This is a television serial about a horse we're casting for! Jesus Christ Superstar, it was *the* audition requirement; it's top priority – we did *say*!'

And Ziggy, I thought in exasperation, you certainly did not say. You failed to mention it because you knew that if you did I would refuse to audition. You knew that I would not lie my way into a part, I would not pretend that I could ride when I could not, even for the female lead in a television serial, especially if it was the prime audition requirement.

But an Equity card was an Equity card.

And I was determined to become an actress.

And so, calling upon all my training at the Rose Jefferson Academy of Dramatic Art, I gave the Casting Director what I hoped was an entirely reassuring smile.

'Of course I can ride,' I said.

2

Love is Just Around the Corner

'I do wish you had let me tell Richard you were coming home this weekend.'

'I hope you didn't.' Across the island of floribundas which divided the lawn from the vegetable patch I looked at my mother suspiciously.

'I didn't, I promise. I just wish I had been allowed to mention it, that's all.' Nipping off a triple dead-head wth her secateurs, she said in a carefully casual tone, 'I have heard that he's been seen around the village with Marcia Cunningham.' On the pretext of tossing the dead-head into the bucket at my feet she straightened in order to observe my reaction. Small, neat, with rosy cheeks, greying hair and shrewd blue eyes, wearing the inevitable green quilted jacket and tweed skirt, my mother was very much the conventional village woman.

Marcia Cunningham. Marcia Cunningham of the pouting lips, the plaintive voice, the luxuriant tumble of red hair combined with the hour-glass figure, the upper part of which was blessed with more than ample proportions. 'Lush' was the adjective one would use to describe Marcia Cunningham. Nevertheless, I was determined not to show any reaction at all.

I shrugged. 'Why shouldn't he see Marcia Cunningham? She's pretty. Her parents are fairly well-to-do. Actually, it's quite a good match.'

The shrewd blue eyes were not entirely convinced. 'Don't you mind?'

I sighed. Parents always meant well, but some things appeared to be quite beyond their comprehension. 'I can't exactly *mind*, can I? I haven't the right to mind. After all, what I'm doing is my own choice, I don't have to do it. If I preferred to stay here, to hang around after Richard Egan, if that was all I wanted out of life then I would, wouldn't I?'

Now it was Mother's turn to sigh. 'I suppose you've found a new beau in London.'

'No, not at all.'

She did not believe me. 'What about Piggy, or whatever his name is?'

'You mean Ziggy. There's nothing between Ziggy and me. Ziggy's just my agent. It's purely a business arrangement.'

'But you're fond of him?'

'Am I? I suppose I am.' I hadn't really thought about it. Nor did I want to think about it. Any kind of personal relationship between agent and client was unprofessional and Ziggy was a professional through and through. There was no chance of emotional entanglement with Ziggy. Nor, if Ziggy had his way, with anyone else whilst I was trying to be an actress. 'You get somebody whispering sweet nothings in your ear then you got to peg it in the opposite direction, Kiddo. You get yourself hooked so you got a choice of priorities and you're running with a stone in your shoe. You're out of the race. You got no chance.'

'You wouldn't approve of Ziggy. You wouldn't consider him at all suitable. He isn't well-connected or wealthy, not like Richard Egan,' I said, 'and by the way, I'm not allowing myself to get too excited about it because I'm not absolutely certain yet, but I think I've got a part.'

'Now what does that mean exactly?' My mother looked at me and her eyebrows were knitted with perplexity.

'It means that I've been offered the female lead in a children's television series written by Tom Sylvester; at least,' I added, wanting to be truthful without launching into explanations about how I'd said I could ride when we both knew perfectly well that I had never sat on a horse in my life, 'provisionally I've been offered it.'

'So you might not get it.'

'I might not. But there's a very good chance that I will.'

From the middle of the floribunda bed the conventional village woman who, before her marriage to my father, had worked as a secretary to a country solicitor and who, after her marriage, had been totally absorbed by her husband, her house, her garden and the belated arrival of her only daughter, and had never been able to understand why that same daughter should aspire to anything different, regarded me with exasperation.

'But every time you come home it's the same old story, Grace,' she said. 'There's always a part on offer, isn't there? There's always a chance that at the next audition, or the one after that there will be a part that's exactly right for you; but it never actually happens, does it? Success is always just around the corner but it's always fractionally out of

18

reach! How many auditions have you been to now? How many months have you been without work?'

'Mother,' I said warningly, 'don't start . . .'

'Soon you will have spent a year of your life without any sort of job. Is it pride that won't allow you to admit that it's hopeless? Why can't you come home, take a secretarial course, and settle down in a proper job?' Angrily she took the head off a rose which was only just coming into flower. 'If your father knew you were living in Finsbury Park with that peculiar landlord, spending your time hanging around Soho and living on Social Security, he would never rest in his grave.'

I had listened to similar tirades many times and knew there was little point in retaliation. Nevertheless: 'That isn't quite fair,' I said, 'and it isn't quite true either. Father encouraged me to go to drama school. He believed I could make it and he wouldn't have wanted me to give up without having a jolly good try. He paid for my training and I mean to give him some return for that. I owe it to him as well as to myself.' As there was no immediate response to this, I added resentfully, 'Crouch End isn't Finsbury Park anyway, it's almost Muswell Hill.'

My mother snipped off a few more dead heads in a resigned sort of way.

'You have never *really* tried to understand me,' I complained. 'You never stop trying to make me see your point of view, but you have never tried to see mine.'

My mother closed her secateurs and snapped on the safety catch. She sighed.

19

'You grumble at me because I don't come home often enough and you grumble at me all the time when I do.'

Mother pushed her way through the floribundas and emerged at my side. In a gesture which was regretful without being in any way apologetic, she handed me the rose she had beheaded by mistake. 'I suppose that after all this time I ought to be able to accept that you are what you are,' she said.

With the bucket of dead-heads we walked back across the lawn towards the cottage which had been my home for the whole of my life.

'You never were an easy child to understand,' my mother said, 'even as an infant.'

'It's too late for me to change now,' I replied.

After supper, whilst Mother settled down with the nine o'clock news, I took Vigor for his evening walk. Vigor was a cross between a spaniel and a collie. He had only one eye, had lost half an ear, and limped. When my father died, Mother had visited a local dog pound to give a home to a stray just as Vigor was being dragged out of his pen towards a final, deadly injection. The dog pound usually managed to find homes for most of its canines, but nobody wanted a dog who had been born in the wild and had almost been reaped by a combine harvester. Vigor's time had run out.

Mother adopted him. By an extraordinary twist of fate, the very imperfections that might have sentenced him to death had at his eleventh hour been his salvation and Vigor, now fit and fully grown, had proved a marvellous companion. Familiarity rendered his Frankenstein looks more endearing than alarming.

I strolled through the village with Vigor bounding ahead, past cottages where nobody bothered to draw their expensive lined curtains; where each interior was much the same as the next, displaying exposed beams, restored inglenook fireplaces, tasteful wall lights; with pretty bone china and old silver standing on good oak furniture; with heavy cut-glass decanters filled with spirits and the palest, dryest sherry. Cottages belonging to respectable people, professional people, qualified, salaried and established people; the sort of people who had dishwashers and wine-racks in their kitchens and Volvos in their garages; people who had proper jobs.

Past the Dog and Badger Inn I walked, where those same professional people were busily downing scotch and gins and tonics at the bar, barking with laughter over trivialities exchanged with acquaintances whose Jaguars and Range Rovers overflowed out of the car park and into the road, then on towards the Rectory and the quiet, secluded, unlit lane beside the church.

It was at this point that Vigor and myself were overtaken by a familiar bright red Porsche 924 whose driver suddenly applied his brakes and came to a halt in a dangerously abrupt manner accompanied by a protesting squeal from the tyres and a shower of displaced gravel.

There was nowhere for me to hide, and in any case it was too late for that.

Richard Egan jumped out of the car. 'Grace!' he exclaimed in a furious voice. 'What on earth are you doing here? You didn't tell me, nobody told me you were expected *this* weekend!'

'Obviously.' I directed a meaningful look towards the passenger seat. Marcia Cunningham gave me a cautious smile which I did not return. I had not wanted to meet Richard or indeed anyone from the village this weekend. I could no longer face their inevitable enquiries about my career. A career which had once seemed to be so assured and was now regarded as something pathetic, a disability even; 'Hello Grace, how's the acting?' couched in a sympathetic tone as if it were shingles or arthritis. I had only agreed to come home to placate my mother, and now I was annoyed to find myself compromised.

I would have walked on, but Richard positioned himself firmly in my path. 'Why the hell didn't you let me know you were coming?' he demanded. 'If I'd known . . .'

'If you'd known,' I said crossly, 'we could have made a jolly threesome, I suppose – you, me and Marcia Cunningham!'

'Don't be a fool. You know that isn't what I meant.'

'I don't think I really care what you meant,' I said. 'Let's get this perfectly clear, Richard. You don't have to apologize to me for being with Marcia, because you are perfectly entitled to be with whoever you like, *perfectly*!'

'And let's get this clear,' he said in a perfectly cold voice, 'I am *not* apologizing.'

'Good,' I snapped, 'because there's no need. I don't care who you go out with.'

'Then why are you so cross?'

'I'm not cross!'

'You are!'

'I am not!'

Vigor came bounding back along the lane. 'Excuse me,' I said politely, 'I have to take my dog for a walk.'

'Not yet,' Richard said firmly. 'Not until we have sorted one or two things out.' He stretched out an arm and took my elbow in a vice-like grip.

'Let me go, Richard,' I told him. 'Let me go. Leave me alone.' I tried to pull away. Richard tightened his grip. 'And anyway,' I reminded him, 'there's Marcia.'

'Yes,' he agreed in a pleasant tone, 'there's always Marcia.' Marcia notwithstanding, he bundled me unceremoniously through the lych-gate and into the shadowy churchyard. Vigor pressed close. He knew Richard as a friend, but was now made wary by the uncertainty of the situation.

'All right, Grace,' Richard said. 'Let's get a few things clear.' As usual he was casually, but immaculately dressed in corduroy trousers, a silk open-necked shirt, a cashmere jersey and a brown leather gilet. And as usual his thick, straight blond hair fell forward over his smoothly handsome face into his heavily lashed blue eyes. No wonder my mother thought him too good to lose. No wonder Marcia Cunningham fancied him. No wonder that, peeved and unsociable as I felt, still I allowed myself to be propelled into the churchyard among the ancient, leaning tombstones, beneath the black and sighing cyprus trees.

'Marcia Cunningham means nothing to me,' Richard declared in a furious voice, '*nothing*!'

'Of course not,' I agreed. 'That's why she's sitting in the passenger seat of your car.'

'If you had condescended to let me know you were coming home this weekend, you know I wouldn't have bothered with her,' he said angrily, 'because you know, and I know, that we have an arrangement.' He moved closer to me, his hands on my shoulders, pushing me towards the church wall.

'Really?' I said innocently. 'What arrangement is that?'

'You know perfectly well what I'm talking about!' My back came into contact with hard stone. Richard was very close now. His breath fanned my face. 'Don't think you can play about with me, Grace. You've known me a long time. You know I always get what I want.'

'Nearly always,' I corrected him.

Vigor growled.

'That's right, boy,' I said in an encouraging tone. 'Kill!'

'Why do you always have to be so difficult, Grace?' Richard's eyes were fathomless pools edged with dark rushes. His mouth breathlessly near, seeking to fasten itself on mine.

'Richard!' Marcia Cunningham's voice called nervously from the lych-gate. 'Richard, are you there?'

Vigor launched himself in the direction of the voice giving tongue with enough volume to do justice to *The Hound of The Baskervilles*. There followed the unmistakable sound of someone falling headlong into gravel. Marcia began to scream.

'*God* Almighty!' Tight-lipped with exasperation,

24

Richard plunged to the rescue across weathered slabs, rusting fleur-de-lis and hummocks of grass.

I might have presumed God to be on my side as, under cover of the church wall, the darkness and the rescue and calming of Marcia Cunningham, I managed to grab Vigor by the scruff of his neck, dragged him out into the lane, and made for home. But Richard was not to be outwitted so easily. He bundled Marcia into the passenger seat and came after me in the car. I ran and Vigor ran, but we were no match for a Porsche 924.

'I'd just like you to know that it's this stupid acting nonsense that's ruining our relationship!' Richard shouted out of his electronic window as I pounded grimly down the lane with Vigor loping lopsidedly at my side. 'If only you'd realize it's just a crazy ego-trip! If only you'd admit it's just a stupid waste of time!'

'Shut up!' I shouted back. 'Shut up and clear off and leave me alone!'

'Give it up, Grace! Come back to Wallingford! For once in your life, see some sense!'

'No!' I yelled. 'No, No, No, NO!'

Abruptly I slowed to a walk. Suddenly there seemed no point in running.

'Grace,' Richard said, 'is this really the way you want it?'

Briefly our eyes met. 'Richard, it's the only way it can be,' I said.

The red Porsche slipped away down the lane. I watched the rear lights fade. Finally they disappeared altogether.

Vigor and I walked on, passing through the other

side of Wallingford. On this side, the council houses were the elite. The scattered cottages improvidently constructed on land which bordered the brook and flooded every winter when the snows melted, were almost derelict. Their walls were cracked and patched with damp, their timbers rotting, their thatch long ago replaced with unsightly corrugated sheeting. Their overgrown gardens were dumping grounds for worn tyres, ancient cookers and rusting bicycles. In this part of Wallingford nobody left their curtains open at night. Every shrunken window was cloaked against prying eyes.

Nobody cares to advertise the fact that they have nothing, I thought. When things don't work out in the way you had hoped, when you can't seem to make a success of things however hard you try, you don't want people to know. You don't come home. You don't want anyone to ask about it. You don't want to see anyone in case they ask. Not even those you love. Sometimes, I thought, especially those you love.

Vigor and I walked the lonely lanes together. The dog with a limp, with only half an ear and one eye, who had been born in the wild and had almost been reaped by a combine harvester, and the girl whose future was not nearly so assured, who wanted desperately to be an actress but who had not worked for almost a year, who hung around Soho and lived on Social Security.

Above us the sky was clear and full of stars. I had never prayed. Even as a child when church attendance had been compulsory, I had never closed my eyes and addressed myself to God. I had been more interested in the earthly ritual, the splendour of my surroundings, the purple and the gold. The rantings from the pulpit, the ceremonials before the altar had been just another theatrical performance to me. Nor could I pray now. But for the first time in my life, I wished that I could. It would have been very handy to have someone omnipotent on my side at a time when things were so frighteningly uncertain. God, I might have said, if you never do another thing for me, give me this part; make *me* a star . . .

3

I Know Where I'm Going . . .

'Horse riding?' Ziggy said when I tackled him about it. 'There's nothing to it. You got something to put your feet in, you got leather reins to hold on to, and away you go. Horse riding's a piece of cake.'

Over the tile-topped table in the corner booth of the Café Marengo I looked at him doubtfully.

One of Ziggy's more successful models, Mickey Gillespie, was sitting with us, waiting to be paid for an assignment. Mickey's chief asset, apart from her elongated and practically fleshless limbs, was her magnificent fall of deep chestnut hair which hung without a kink or a split end to the small of her back. She commented, 'I had to do some pictures on a white horse in a poppy field once, and I didn't think it was a piece of cake. I felt ever such a long way off the ground and I didn't half rock about; if my horse had gone faster than a walk I'd have fallen straight off.'

'That's because you don't have the balance, Kiddo,' Ziggy told her. 'That's because you didn't do the stage school bit and missed out on the fencing and dancing and stuff like that. Grace Darling'll take to riding like a duck to water; all you got to do is think of the horse as a furry bicycle.'

Even I, who had never mounted so much as a beach donkey, thought this an over-simplification, but any immediate objection was forestalled by the arrival of a tall, large-bosomed girl with startlingly blue eyes and thick white-blonde hair sliced to the level of her earlobes. The blue eyes appraised and dismissed Mickey and myself and came to rest on Ziggy, who was slouched in his habitual manner over half a cup of cold cappuccino, his enormous thick silver identity bracelet dangling from his wrist, his black leather blouson with the appliqué silver star draped over his shoulder, and his bleached hair showing dark at the roots.

'Are you Ziggy Stanislavski?' she wanted to know. 'Because if you are, you did say eleven o'clock.'

Ziggy looked up at her in a leisurely manner. 'Eleven o'clock I did say,' he conceded. 'You Emma Hall?'

Emma Hall nodded. 'Jerry Martin rang you about me. I want to get into West End musicals. Jerry said you would hear me.'

'Sure I'll hear you.' Ziggy leaned back against the plastic padding of the bench seat and gave the new arrival his fullest attention. His shrewd blue eyes travelled every inch of Emma Hall, taking in every detail of her appearance, the way she was built, the way she carried herself, registering her self-possessed manner and the way she put her clothes together, the image she presented. And yet I knew that the quality Ziggy valued most in his clients was invisible to the naked eye. What Ziggy was looking for was grit. 'Acting is no baby park, Kiddo,' he had warned when I had first met him. 'Maybe you got the looks, the talent, the training, but if you ain't got the grit, you ain't going nowhere. You got the red light before you got into first gear.'

Now he looked approvingly at Emma Hall. 'Well, you definitely got the right build for it, Blue Eyes,' he said. 'You got the height, you got the shoulders, you got a well-developed chest. You certainly got room in there for resonating spaces.'

Emma Hall did not know quite how to take this. 'Oh yes,' she said. She frowned slightly.

'You're easy on the eye, you got style, you got presence,' Ziggy said. 'On the West End stage you'd be a knockout.'

'Do you really think so?' Emma Hall's voice was hopeful but she was not completely taken in. I could see suspicion in the blue eyes and I was glad for her sake.

'Only trouble is,' continued Ziggy, 'twenty thousand others got the same, so you better have a voice in there, Blue Eyes, else you lost an oar before you got to the regatta.'

'I can sing,' she said crossly, 'if that's what you mean.'

'OK,' Ziggy said with equanimity, 'let's hear it.'

The beautiful blue eyes widened. Emma Hall looked at Ziggy, then at Mickey and me, then she looked round at the scattering of patrons in the booths and on the counter stools of the Café Marengo. 'You mean now?' she asked in an incredulous tone. '*Here*?'

Ziggy shrugged. 'It's not the Albert Hall, I grant you, but you got to start somewhere.'

'Well, I know *that*,' she said, 'but . . .'

'Listen, Blue Eyes,' Ziggy said, 'if you can't trill a bar in front of half a dozen people, you can forget the West End.'

30

'It isn't that I don't have the nerve,' Emma Hall snapped, 'it's just that I hardly expected . . .'

'I don't care what you expected,' Ziggy said. 'You can expect what you like, there's no charge for expectation, but my time's expensive, so you can either trill me a bar or toddle off back to Jerry Martin and tell him you flunked it.'

Emma Hall glared at him. For a moment she looked as if she was about to leave. Then suddenly she straightened up, cleared her throat, took a breath and pitched into the audition song from 'Stage Fright' with enormous determination.

She certainly had resonance chambers. I had never heard anything as loud in my life. Nor, to judge by his startled expression, had Ziggy. Emma Hall's voice could have filled every last inch of the Albert Hall without the benefit of amplifying equipment.

> *'I know*
> *Where I'm going*
> *Don't think*
> *I'll give up and go away,*
> *I'm here to stay!'*

All of the patrons seated on the counter stools turned as one man. Heads popped up over the top of the booths to see what was going on.

> *'Pick me up and shake me*
> *Test me to my limits, break me,*
> *Make it as tough as you can make it –*
> *I can take it!*

The proprietor of the Café Marengo, Mr Vincinelli, flew out from behind his espresso machine

31

and gesticulated in a panic-stricken way behind the soloist. '*Please*, Mr Stanislavski,' he shouted, 'you must have some consideration for my customers!'

> '*You think*
> *I'm a loser –*
> *But nobody believed*
> *I'd even get this far;*
> *I'll be a star!*'

Rather abruptly the performance was over. Emma Hall stared at Ziggy defiantly. Ziggy swallowed a few times and tapped his ears in an experimental manner, like an air traveller suffering altitude pressure. 'Well, Blue Eyes,' he acknowledged, 'you certainly got the volume.'

'Mr Stanislavski,' said Mr Vincinelli in a severe voice, 'I have to tell you that if this happen one more time I charge you double for rent of my table.'

'Double my rent?' Ziggy said, scandalized. 'When I give your customers free entertainment?'

Mr Vincinelli walked back to his counter like a man with a headache.

'Well,' Emma Hall demanded, 'what do you think?'

'I think you got to take singing lessons,' Ziggy said.

'I've *had* singing lessons,' she said crossly. 'I've been having singing lessons for the last six years of my life!'

'Take more singing lessons,' Ziggy replied. 'Go away. Go get a day job in a nice shop. Get singing lessons four nights a week. Come back in six months.'

'Six months!' Emma Hall stared at him, appalled.

'On the other three nights,' Ziggy went on, 'get dancing lessons.'

'Now listen to me, Ziggy Stanislavski,' Emma Hall said angrily, 'I've had dancing lessons and I've had singing lessons. I've had dancing and singing lessons until I'm blue in the face. I'm sick of lessons. Lessons won't get me anywhere; what I need is stage experience.'

'And you listen to me, Blue Eyes,' Ziggy said. 'You want to be on the West End stage, then you get singing lessons four nights and dancing lessons three nights, and in six months you come back and we'll try again. Otherwise forget it.'

Emma Hall looked as though she might launch herself across the table and punch him on the nose, then suddenly the façade of self-assurance crumbled and her blue eyes were flooded with disappointment. 'Oh rats,' she said, 'am I really that bad?'

'You're not as good as you got to be,' Ziggy told her, 'and that's a fact.'

Somehow she managed to cope with this, controlling her breath and her emotion as only a singer can, straightening her drooping shoulders, catching her bottom lip with her teeth. 'OK,' she said, 'thanks for hearing me.' She turned and made for the door.

'And Blue Eyes,' Ziggy called after her, 'in your lunch hours take acting lessons!' Having delivered this parting shot he called for three cappuccinos.

'Is it really necessary to be so hard on people,' I wondered. 'I thought her voice was terrific.'

'Sure it's terrific,' he said, 'lots of voices are terrific. I got terrific voices calling up orders in

MacDonalds right now. What d'you want me to tell her, Kiddo? Do I say the West End's eating its heart out for her terrific voice when I know there's a famine out there? When there's already twenty thousand starving in the queue? Sure she's got a voice, but I got nothing for her and a few more lessons won't do any harm. If she's a stayer, she'll be back before six months, and then maybe there'll be something and maybe there won't.'

Mickey who would have much preferred to be a singer than a model, said wistfully, 'If I had a voice like that, I'd *really* be going places.'

'Listen Kiddo, the only place you're going is back to that crooked agency to pay them off.' Ziggy dug into his money belt and extracted a wad of notes which he proceeded to count out on to the table. When Mickey had come out of Modelling School she had done the usual tour of the agencies with her portfolio, starting with the well-known ones, working down via the less well-known to the frankly dubious where, like hundreds of would-be models before her, she had been ripped off. The agency had enthused about her looks, and promised to find her work but criticized her portfolio and dispatched her to a nearby studio to have a new set of photographs taken. Naturally, the photographer had been on the payroll and there was no work to be had, but Mickey had been presented with a bill for two hundred and thirty pounds for a new, and grossly inferior portfolio. This kind of thing was happening all the time for there was always a fresh supply of innocents; would-be dancers, singers, models, actors and actresses coming out of the schools, believing that they had something special to offer. 'Without somebody who knows the business you're just babes in the wood,' Ziggy maintained, and already I had seen enough to know that he was right.

'Three hundred quid, less fifty is two hundred and fifty,' Ziggy said finally, pushing a pile of notes across the tiles to Mickey, 'and you make sure you get a receipt because I'll be checking, so don't go blowing this little lot down Oxford Street.'

'Hey, wait a minute,' Mickey objected, 'what do you mean three hundred less fifty? I may be a little lacking in the upper storey in your estimation, Zig, but I can work out percentages, and I know ten per cent of three hundred isn't fifty quid!'

'OK, Gillespie, look at it this way. Thirty quid commission. Fifteen quid I shelled to get your hair fixed, and five quid so you could buy a pizza – I got it all in the book . . .'

'Don't bother with the book,' Mickey said hastily, 'I'd forgotten about the hair and the pizza.'

'Just don't forget to pay off the agency, Kiddo.'

'I won't.'

'Now Grace Darling,' Ziggy turned his attention to me. 'You got to go do a film test. It's not something you get cooked about, it's a formality, but you got to do it because they need to get you on film.'

This was the first I had heard of it. 'Why?' I asked. 'What for?'

'I told you, they got to take some shots, they have to see how you look on film. After that they can tell you lose some weight, grow your hair a couple more inches, get your teeth fixed.'

'There's nothing wrong with my teeth,' I said. 'I've had them fixed.'

'I'm just telling you why they need the shots.' Ziggy paused in order to receive the cappuccino from Mr Vincinelli who appeared more than usually agitated and had over-steamed the milk so that the froth stood up in mountainous peaks.

One felt that Mr Vincinelli, who had a love-hate relationship with Ziggy, spent his time behind the espresso machine composing his latest complaint against Ziggy's 'artistes' and sure enough: 'Mr Stanislavski,' he began in a wounded tone, 'last week I ask you to invite no more tap dancing ladies to my café because of damage to my floors, and now I ask you, I *beg* you, please to invite no more singing persons because for this I need special licence from the police, and it is quite possible that you make many troubles for me in my business.'

'The only troubles I make for you in your business,' Ziggy said, spooning raw cane sugar over the exaggerated froth on his cappuccino, 'is if I split. If you got a legitimate complaint, Vincinelli, I got to listen, but you know and I know that your customers like my auditions, and if I go, they go.'

Mr Vincinelli walked back to his counter, temporarily defeated.

'At this film test, Grace Darling,' Ziggy continued, 'you get to meet your co-star.'

'Co-star?' I had not even considered my co-star. I had been too preoccupied with the prospect of having to ride a horse. 'Who is he? Do you know who he is?'

Ziggy shook his head. 'I got no information on

that score, Kiddo, except that he'll be six feet otherwise you wouldn't have got the part.'

The thought of a co-star immediately made me feel inadequate. What would happen if we did not agree, if we disliked each other on sight? Such things did happen, I knew, and to people of proven ability who were already well-known and famous for their work. The odds were rather stacked against two novices, both out to make an impression, who had neither the ability nor the confidence to be generous in their work.

Worse, what if my co-star turned out to be an established television actor? Would he despise me for my youth and inexperience? I was sure that he would. How could he possibly respect someone who, apart from training videos and the fumbling efforts of the 'techies', the stage management students at drama school, had never before faced the cameras. I could imagine myself, flushed with hopeless embarrassment, sweating in the heat from the lights, mumbling, forgetting my lines, losing control of my hands and my feet, knowing that the camera crew were trying not to laugh at my discomforture, that the Director was boiling with rage, and somehow worse than anything that Tom Sylvester, who had seen two hundred and twenty-seven females without a flicker of an eyelid before deciding to take me, was looking on balefully from inside the collar of his anorak.

'And so, Grace Darling,' Ziggy said, 'you got to go to Whipps Common Thursday morning, ten A.M. sharp.'

As a location for a film test, the absurdity of it

37

jerked me out of my speculations. 'Whipps *Common*?'

'Location shots, Kiddo. The great outdoors. It's a horse story, remember; you won't be shooting in studio – you got to have your hair blowing in the breeze.'

I supposed that was reasonable, if rather unexpected and nerve-wracking. 'But Ziggy,' I reminded him, 'it's the riding I'm really worried about. I'm just terrified that when they find out I can't do it, they'll re-audition for the part.'

'Listen, Kiddo,' Ziggy said patiently, 'you're cooked about the riding even though I tell you there's nothing to it. I tell you what – ' he produced a ten pound note from his money belt and pushed it across the table, ' – go get yourself a lesson.'

It was very generous of him, but, 'One?' I said faintly.

'Have a heart, Grace Darling,' Ziggy said. 'You don't need more than one. One horse riding lesson's enough for anybody.'

4

No Time to Love You

'One day
When I am famous
When I am
Fêted everywhere, known,
And wanted;
Too high on my cloud to regret you,
I'll forget you.

The room next to mine had been unoccupied for weeks, but now the clear, emotion-charged voice of a singer rang through the wall which, for all its fussily patterned wallpaper and framed theatrical handbills, was little more than a hardboard partition.

It was not that I minded the singing. There was precious little peace and quiet to be had at Henry Irving House, N8, anyway, but I could have wished for something a little less ironic. Henry Irving House was supported by a little known Arts Trust Fund which meant that drama, model, and music school graduates could apply for one year of subsidised accommodation at the end of their training, which gave them one year in affordable, sheltered housing whilst they looked for work. I did not need to be reminded by the lyrics of 'Stage Fright' that all of us at Henry Irving House were waiting to be famous, clinging desperately to hope, acting our heads off in the daylight hours to keep up a confident façade. But oh, when one lay in the darkness of one's own little room at night, how quickly the façade crumbled away. Doubts and fears stood waiting in the shadows to crowd around the bedside like a Victorian family called to a dying relative. Self-doubt, gloom and anxiety were familiar night time visitors to my bedside, and now a part was actually in the offing, terror of losing it stood beside them.

Over and over again I had relived the audition; seeing again the Casting Director's harassed expression, and the way Tom Sylvester had opened one eye, then two eyes, and the way he had zipped up his anorak and capered away across the dusty floor after saying he would make me a star without even asking to hear me read a script. Was it possible that an important television part could be decided in such an eccentric fashion? I did not know. But the following day my riding lesson was booked, and the day after that I was to attend the film test on Whipps Common. Every time I thought about it my stomach twisted into a painful knot. I tried hard not to think about it at all.

'Telephone for Miss Vincent!' Above the lyrics of 'Stage Fright', the voice of Lancelot, Henry Irving's landlord shrilled. I went out on to the landing with my heart in my mouth, praying that it wasn't Ziggy ringing to tell me the whole thing had been called off.

Outside my room, typical Henry Irving pandemonium reigned. In her room on the opposite side of the landing Mickey was working out to the accompaniment of a record. Lancelot, clad in a pink jump-suit and one dangling earring rapped on her door. 'Not so LOUD, darling! Turn the volume DOWN! I tell you, it's *bedlam* out here!'

On the staircase, two young men wearing visors and flourishing fencing foils were practising parries and thrusts. I dodged past them with Lancelot tripping behind me. 'Very laudable dears, very, but not on my stairs in you *don't* mind. It's very inconvenient for the other tenants and I do have to think about the Wilton.'

One of the young men held off his opponent long enough to glance down at the stair-treads. 'Come off it, Lancelot. Some of us do know what Wilton looks like. This haircord rubbish is so old it's practically historic.'

In the hall I retrieved the dangling telephone receiver.

'Grace? Is that you?' It was Richard's voice.

'Yes.' Relief that it was not Ziggy ringing to tell me that Tom Sylvester had changed his mind soon turned to exasperation. I was far too fraught to think about Richard, and I certainly did not want to talk to him. I had far too many important things on my mind. 'What do you want?' I asked in an unwelcoming tone. 'I'm rather busy at the moment.'

'Busy doing what?' Richard countered. 'I was under the impression you were unemployed.'

I gritted my teeth. From the foot of the staircase Lancelot was trilling, 'Then go and practise in the street, jump up and down the kerb, use your imagination, but not on my haircord *if* you don't mind!'

'Grace?' Richard demanded, 'are you still there?'

'Yes,' I said, 'I'm still here.'

The front door banged shut behind the fencing partners.

'There are times,' Lancelot remarked to me in passing, 'when one looks at the type of person coming into the dramatic arts and is *racked* with concern for the future of the profession.'

'Now look here, Grace,' Richard said firmly. 'We have to talk.'

> *'One day*
> *I'll be up there*
> *with the stars*
> *Everyone will know me*
> *I will be so far above you*
> *There will be no time*
> *To love you.'*

The singer had now added a taped musical accompaniment. The clear voice soared. Lancelot stiffened. He went back up the staircase.

'What would you like to talk about?' I inquired. 'Your most recent outing with Marcia Cunningham?'

'I haven't been out with Marcia Cunningham since the weekend,' Richard said.

'What a pity. Why don't you ask her out this evening?'

'I already have.'

'Then why bother to ring me?' I snapped.

Lancelot's voice floated down the stairs. 'Sweetheart, it's beautiful, it wrings my heart, but it's very *loud . . .*'

'What do you expect me to do, Grace?' Richard said in a furious voice. 'Sit here on my backside waiting for you to condescend to inform me you are coming home for one weekend out of six?'

'You know that isn't what I expect,' I said crossly. '*I* haven't the right to expect anything! I thought I had already made it clear that I'm not free to make any sort of commitment, I'm not ready for the kind of relationship you want. I have to put my career first!'

'And what career is that, for heaven's sake? You haven't *got* a career, Grace! You're just fooling yourself!'

After all the agonized uncertainty of the last few days this was simply too much to take. 'What on *earth* do you know about my career?' I demanded. 'What makes you fit to judge?'

The front door of Henry Irving House opened and the fencing partners came into the hall, pulling off their visors, shaking rain off their clothes.

'I know a damn sight more about earning a living than you do,' Richard said in an arctic voice.

'But not through your own efforts,' I reminded him angrily. 'Not because of anything *you've* done! Only because you were handed your father's business on a silver plate! You've *never* had to struggle in your life! You don't know the first thing about building a career, so don't think you're so blooming clever!'

The fencing partners paused at the foot of the staircase, interested.

'If you'd been a halfwit you would still be where you are,' I raged on, 'running the family business, drawing a fat wage packet, driving a Porsche! So don't think any of that qualifies you to criticize *my* efforts because it flaming well doesn't!'

Lancelot, halfway down the staircase, gave me a

reproachful look over the banister rail. 'Temper, darling,' he warned.

'I think you had better stop there, Grace.' Richard's voice was pure ice. 'I really see no point in continuing this conversation.'

'Right!' I cried. 'You're absolutely right!' I threw the telephone receiver back into its cradle. I leaned my head against the wall. I was shaking with rage. I felt terrible.

Lancelot tripped down the stairs and shooed away the fencing partners. He was all sympathy. 'Come and sit down in my dear little flat,' he suggested. 'I'll open a bottle of my nicest wine and we can watch *Dynasty* together and be pleasurably appalled.'

'No, thank you,' I sniffed. 'It's very kind of you, Lancelot – most kind; but honestly, I couldn't.'

'I can't say I blame you,' he agreed.

Back in my tiny bedroom I sat down on my divan and tried to convince myself that if I never saw or heard from Richard Egan again, it would be to my advantage.

> *'But one day*
> *When it is all over*
> *When I am*
> *No longer lovely, nor young,*
> *Nor wanted,*
> *When the only stars are high above me,*
> *Who will love me?'*

I put my head under my pillow. It was not that I minded the singing, it was the lyrics that got on my nerves. Not only that, but I suddenly realized that I recognized the voice. It belonged to Emma Hall.

5

Pine Kernels are not Onions

'I think you were barmy to choke him off like that. I mean, you've only got a few weeks left at Henry Irving, and say this TV part don't come off and nothing else turns up? You'll have to go home for a bit to scrape up enough cash for a deposit on a room, so what's the point of kicking a rich young fella like him in the teeth just when you need cheering up?'

'I don't actually think of Richard as a rich young fella,' I said. 'I've known him for years. His father and my father were at school together. I wouldn't dream of going out with him just because it happened to be convenient.'

'Well, I reckon you should,' Mickey decided. 'And what's more, I reckon you should keep him around as a future prospect for the marriage stakes. You'll probably end up marrying somebody after all, and you don't want to get hitched to any actors because they're all mixed up before they start. You've got to use your loaf, Grace. Think of the *security*. Think of the *money*.'

I looked at her in exasperation. 'Security isn't *everything*,' I said. 'Money isn't *everything*.' It was all very well for Mickey to dish out advice about men. She hated them. In her short career she had been taken advantage of so many times that she had developed an aversion to the opposite sex which amounted to a serious psychological hang-up. Since I had known her she had never had a date, and there had often been problems on modelling assignments because any form of physical contact repelled her. In spite of this, at times I suspected even because of it, Ziggy kept her on, and whenever possible teamed her with male models who were known to be homosexual.

'You'll be glad of money and security one day,' she said, 'and Richard Egan's offer might be the best you'll get.'

'He hasn't actually *made* an offer,' I pointed out.

'But he will,' she said in a confident tone, 'just you wait.'

We were sharing a cheap meal in a Crouch End café and the waitress crashed a pizza tin on to our table in a bad-tempered way. Chiefly due to Mickey's spectacular looks, our table was attracting the attention of the male clientcle whose admiration she obviously considered her own exclusive province. Our pizza had taken an unusually long time to arrive and we had long ago finished our side-salads. I had not eaten all day and watched avidly as Mickey flourished the serving knife.

'Wait a minute,' Emma Hall said in a commanding voice. 'Don't cut it yet, she's given us onions.'

'So what?' Mickey wanted to know. 'Who cares?'

'I do.' Emma pulled the pizza tin out of range of the serving knife in a pre-emptive manner. 'I've got a singing lesson tonight and I can't breathe onions all over my tutor.' She called the waitress back to the table. 'We didn't order onions,' she informed her. 'Mushrooms and pine kernels, we said. You've given us onions.'

The waitress gave her a look of hatred and snatched up the tin. She flung it back on to the counter and there followed an altercation with the pizza cook which involved many venomous glances towards our table.

'I don't think pizza onions are all that strong,' I objected, anguished by the sensation of being within a hair's breadth of a meal, only to have it snatched from beneath my nose. 'Couldn't you have scraped them off your portion, or sucked a peppermint before your lesson? Are onions instead of pine kernels really such an issue? I'm absolutely *starving*.'

'So am I,' Emma agreed, 'but it isn't just because of the singing lesson, it's really a matter of principle.'

Mickey gave me a vengeful look. She had not been enthusiastic about my proposal to invite Emma in the first place. Now that we faced another interminable wait for a fresh pizza, she was even less enthusiastic. It did seem a high price to pay for someone else's principle.

'Pine kernels are not onions,' Emma insisted, 'just as coffee is not tea, and potatoes are not tomatoes. There is no point in ordering from a menu if the staff can then serve whatever happens to be convenient. That pizza was probably a cancelled order.'

'I'd settle for a cancelled order instead of a principle any day,' Mickey grumbled.

Emma ignored her. 'Richard Egan is also a matter of principle,' she announced.

'Really?' I looked at her, interested.

'Most certainly. You were absolutely right to say

what you did. You can't afford a relationship with someone like that.'

'Well, *that's* a load of rubbish,' Mickey interjected. 'If you ask me, Grace can't afford *not* to have a relationship with somebody like that.'

'But then Grace wasn't asking you,' Emma said, 'she was asking me.'

'I wasn't aware that I had asked either of you,' I said hastily, 'and don't think I'm not grateful for your interest, but there isn't much more to be said about Richard. He won't try to contact me again.'

'Of course he will,' Mickey scoffed. 'Now you've torn him off a strip, he'll be keener than ever.'

'You may think so,' I said, 'but then you don't know Richard.' And I did know Richard. And I remembered the icy chill of his voice when he had said, 'I think you had better stop there, Grace. I see no point in continuing this conversation.' And I knew only too well how the jaw would have tightened, how the mouth would have compressed into a line, how the beautiful blue eyes would have hardened into flint. No, I knew Richard, and I knew he would not contact me again. I had burned my boats there.

'Well, if he doesn't try again that will be good news,' Emma decided. 'Because if you're really serious about your career, Grace, you have to give up all close relationships, *especially* with people who try to discourage you.'

'Now wait a minute,' I said. 'There's no doubt in my mind that I'm totally serious about my career, but I wouldn't be so quick to criticize Richard for trying to discourage me – all he knows is that I'm out of work and miserable.'

'There you go,' Mickey said in a satisfied voice, 'now you're sticking up for him. I knew you were mad about him really.'

'I am *not* mad about Richard Egan,' I insisted.

'Yes you are.' Mickey could be very irritating at times.

'Well, if you are mad about him, it could be very damaging for your career,' Emma said in a censorious tone.

'What career?' I asked grumpily.

'Well, there's the television serial, for a start.'

'If I get it,' I said. 'I have the film test to get through first, and after that, there's the little matter of the horse riding . . .' The knowledge that I had burned my boats with Richard, the uncertainty about the television part, and the hunger gnawing away at my stomach made me feel depressed and irritable. I wished I had not suggested coming out. I wished I had stayed at Henry Irving with a Pot Noodle and a mug of coffee. At Henry Irving I could be depressed in peace, without having to share the cost of a pizza I could not really afford with people I liked less with every passing minute.

'I think you should pull yourself together, Grace,' Emma advised, 'because even if you lose this part, you can't allow yourself to be defeated. You just have to try harder for the next. You just have to get in there and make it happen.'

Career counselling from someone who hadn't even managed to find herself an agent was the last thing I wanted. 'I've been out there trying to make it happen for eleven months,' I reminded her tartly.

She shrugged. 'Maybe it will take another eleven months.'

'Now she sounds just like Ziggy,' Mickey commented.

'There are worse people to sound like. I've heard he's a very good agent. I'm going to get on his books,' Emma announced.

Such confidence was very irksome. 'Ziggy's books are full,' I said. 'He won't take you.'

'He will,' Emma said. 'Because I'm going to make him.'

At this moment a loutish youth on an adjacent table leaned back on his chair in order to tweak one of the endless locks of Mickey's hair. In an instant she had whipped round with the pizza knife in her hand. 'If you do that again,' she told him, 'I'll slit your throat.'

His face froze. 'Now hold on there,' he protested. 'It were only meant to be a joke.'

'I don't joke,' Mickey snapped. 'Not with people I don't know.' She returned the knife calmly to the table. 'If I don't get something to eat soon, I'm going to have to start on the plastic flowers.' She took a purple anemone from the arrangement in the centre of the table and stuck it in her hair.

'Now you'll just attract more attention than ever,' Emma pointed out, 'although if you don't enjoy the attention, I wonder why you wear such exotic clothes.'

'Exotic?' Mickey frowned.

'Well – ' With supreme tactlessness, Emma corrected herself. ' – What I really meant to say was provocative.'

'*Provocative*?' Mickey glared at Emma. Surreptitiously I removed the pizza knife to my side of the table. 'Are you saying I go around indecently dressed?'

'Not indecently dressed exactly,' Emma tried to explain. 'All I mean is that you should wear slightly less . . .'

'She couldn't wear any less,' I interrupted in an unhelpful way, 'otherwise she wouldn't be wearing anything at all.' This was true. Mickey was currently wearing a skimpy, shrunken jersey that barely covered her midriff and a mini-skirt she had constructed herself out of a wash-leather.

'I didn't mean less clothes,' Emma said irritably. 'What I was going to say was a little less eye-catching clothes.'

'What you mean,' Mickey flared, 'is that I should cover myself up so that nobody notices me!'

'One pizza *without* onions!' What could have been a full scale row was mercifully arrested by the bad-tempered waitress who dropped the new pizza tin on to the table. The prospect of food instantly restored everyone's humour.

'You've got a point in a way, I suppose,' Mickey acknowledged as she drove the serving knife by way of pine kernels, mushrooms, cheese and tomato paste into the crust. 'I don't expect I really mind being stared at, otherwise I wouldn't be a model, would I?' She slid a piece of pizza, trailing strings of creamy mozzarella, on to a plate.

'And we all want to be noticed in our different ways,' I added, 'otherwise we wouldn't be struggling along, waiting for the world to recognize our talents.'

'That's true,' Emma agreed, graciously accepting the first slice of pizza as her due. 'In a way, we must all have a touch of egotistical masochism in our make-up.'

'Perhaps we should call and see the pharmacist on the way home,' Mickey suggested. 'He might have pills for it.'

With enormous relief, I took the next plate. 'Either that, or we could change to Helena Rubenstein,' I said.

6

In My Profession . . .

In retrospect, no lesson at all would have been preferable to one. I had found a riding school in a tiny London mews near Hyde Park, where the stables were Edwardian and multi-story, with access to the upper block by way of a steep ramp with the cobblestones offset to allow the horses purchase on the slope. No one walking past the entrance would have noticed it, but inside the yard one could almost have imagined oneself in the country. The sound of the traffic faded, horses looked over their half-doors, chickens scratched, a coal black cat lay stretched out on a bale of straw. A girl polishing a brown horse with a cloth as if it was a piece of good mahogany furniture, pointed out the office.

I was no more than a few seconds late, but already my instructress showed signs of impatience. Miss Evelyn Trubshawe was wide and weathered, with a brusque manner and an unforgiving eye. She was dressed entirely in black – black boots, black breeches, black jersey and a black leather gilet. Her greying hair was scraped back into a bun which was imprisoned in a black slumber net, and she was holding a whip several feet taller than herself which had a formidable thong to it, ending with a few knots and a little red lash. I was already feeling nervous and my nerves increased when I saw Miss

Evelyn Trubshawe. She looked like a gaoler in a particularly depressing film about the Nazi regime.

She looked me up and down in disbelief. 'This is it then, is it?' she said in a dry tone. 'This is your idea of riding kit?'

Nervous though I was, I did not allow myself to be intimidated. My pink and beige jersey, worn with jeans, pink leg-warmers and stiletto heels may not have been ideal, but at least I had taken the trouble to enquire what I should wear when I had booked my lesson.

'I was told I didn't need special riding kit for a single lesson,' I said. 'When I made the appointment they just said I should wear something to protect my legs, and to be sure to wear shoes with heels.'

Miss Trubshawe looked at my footwear. She gave a snort of disgust. 'In this profession, shoes with heels mean heels like this.' With the end of the hideous whip she tapped the heel of her black rubber boot.

'And in my profession,' I said, 'shoes with heels mean heels like this.' I lifted a foot and tapped my stiletto.

Miss Trubshawe compressed her lips and gave me a steely look. She was not about to enquire what my profession was, but I could tell she had already classified it as disreputable.

'Come with me.' In a resigned manner she now stumped out into the yard and I followed. In a room filled with saddles and bridles and smelling pungently of leather, oil and soap, Miss Trubshawe propped up her whip and threw open the lid of a vast tin trunk. As she leaned over and delved into it, I rather hoped her black breeches would burst at the seams to punish her for not being the warm, sympathetic instructress I had envisaged, but the stitching held fast.

From the depths of the trunk were produced a pair of rubber boots similar to Miss Trubshawe's own. They were a size six but even so were difficult to get on, and I was forced to abandon the pink leg-warmers. Next, I was handed a shiny black hat with perforated earpieces, a plastic peak, and a complicated harness including a chin-cup, which Miss Trubshaw personally strapped around my jaw.

'There,' she said with grim satisfaction. 'That's a bit more like it. That's better.'

I did not think it was better. The hat felt most uncomfortable. There was a long glass display case on one wall of the room, which contained rosettes and prize cards. I could see my reflection in it. I only needed Ziggy's leather blouson to pass for a motor cycle despatch rider.

'Is this hat really necessary?' I wanted to know. Somehow the image in the display case did not quite match the way I had envisaged myself looking on horseback. In the romantic films of my youth, people had galloped into the sunset with their hair streaming out behind them, and as far as I knew, they still did – in chocolate and fashion advertisements, at least.

'The hat is not only necessary, it is compulsory.' Miss Trubshawe slammed down the lid of the trunk. She grasped her whip and marched out of the door. I trailed behind, furtively tugging at the straps on the chin harness, trying to loosen them.

Out in the yard the girl who had been polishing

the mahogany horse was now holding another, this one small and fat, and brown and white in patches, with a mane that stood stiff and upright like a punk's hairstyle.

'Oh,' I said. 'Is this mine?' I was a little disappointed as I would have much preferred the mahogany horse. This solid, rather common little horse, with his odd markings and his white eyelashes, looked as if he would be more at home trotting behind a Romany caravan.

'It is.' The tone of Miss Trubshaw's voice intimated that this was the horse's misfortune and not mine. Considering that the half hour lesson was about to cost me eight pounds, I thought she might have been more civil, but I consoled myself with the thought that if I managed to grasp the basic principles of riding in thirty minutes, lack of civility would be a small price to pay, and may even turn out to be an advantage. Miss Evelyn Trubshawe was not the sort of instructress to waste valuable time in social chit-chat.

The girl now attached a long piece of webbing called a lungeing rein to a ring on the horse's cavesson. I knew all about lungeing reins and cavessons because with the two pounds I had left of Ziggy's ten, I had bought myself a paperback book entitled *All About Horses and Horse Riding*. Because of *All About Horses and Horse Riding* I now noticed that there were no stirrup leathers and irons on the saddle.

'Where are the stirrup irons?' I said.

'There are no stirrup irons,' said Miss Trubshaw.

Then I noticed that there were no proper reins on

the bridle. I could see a rein clipped on to the bit, but instead of the buckled end lying at the bottom of the stiff little mane, ready for me to take hold of, it disappeared under the saddle.

'Where are the reins?' I said.

'There are no reins,' said Miss Trubshaw.

'But how am I going to learn to ride without stirrups and reins?' I demanded.

Miss Trubshaw was tightening the girths on the saddle. She gave me a look which indicated that not only did she consider me disreputable and unworthy of her attention, but also brainless as well. 'When you can ride without reins and stirrups, you will be given reins and stirrups,' she snapped.

This did not altogether make sense to me. I wondered if there was a shortage of reins and stirrups, if the riding school had somehow run out of them. And yet I had seen lots of them in the tackroom. From *All About Horses and Horse Riding*, I had learned how to hold the reins, that the rein entered the fist at the little finger and came out between the index finger and the thumb, and that the ball of the foot rested on the tread of the stirrup, and now I felt rather cheated to be so unexpectedly deprived of both. I wondered if, without the provision of reins and stirrups, I would actually be getting my money's worth in this riding lesson. Or to be strictly accurate, Ziggy's money's worth.

It seemed profitless to raise objections with someone like Miss Trubshawe. I decided to introduce myself to my horse. I went up to it and patted its neck. It felt rather coarse, but warm to the touch.

The horse did not appear to notice my friendly overture. It did not seem at all interested in making my acquaintance. In fact, it appeared to be practically asleep. The white-fringed eyes were half-closed and the pink lower lip drooped in a languorous manner. Not a muscle stirred as I stroked the brown and white face.

'He isn't very friendly, is he?' I said to the girl.

She looked rather startled, as if expecting a horse to be friendly was an entirely new idea. 'Pedro isn't unfriendly,' she said, 'and you would hardly expect him to fall all over you and lick your boots – he isn't a dog, after all.'

'I suppose not,' I said. But it was unsatisfactory all the same, not to have any kind of acknowledgment.

'Follow me, Miss Vincent.' Miss Trubshawe now took charge of the coiled-up lungeing rein. Instantly, Pedro opened his eyes. He walked across the yard, shoulder-to-shoulder with Miss Trubshawe like an old friend. He was not in the least bit worried by the hideous whip with its swinging thong. He looked a different animal, cheerful, energetic, altogether too jaunty. In retrospect I had liked him a lot better when he was asleep.

Now that the time had almost come to mount, I was frightened. My heart had started to bump against my ribs in an uncomfortable way, and my palms felt damp. Unwillingly I walked behind Pedro and Miss Trubshawe as they crossed the yard and passed under an archway set into the multi-storey stable block. On the other side of the archway was a fenced lungeing circle which looked rather like a circus ring. The surface was soft and springy under-foot. One could have been walking in a pine forest where centuries of falling needles had made the ground resilient.

'Bark,' Miss Trubshawe informed me.

In my anxiety I looked at her, startled, not under-standing. 'Sorry?'

'Bark,' she explained. 'The surface is made of bark chippings. It makes for a soft landing.'

I hoped this was intended as a joke. Uneasily, I watched as Miss Trubshawe tightened the girth straps under the saddle flaps. Pedro flipped his ears back and swished his tail, not enjoying it.

Unusually for a village child, I had never had any contact with ponies. To me the equine species were merely useful props in the western and period films I watched at the cinema and on the television. Marcia Cunningham had ridden, certainly. I could remember seeing her ride along the village street, proud and top-heavy on a fat bay pony. Richard, I recalled with a pang, had also owned ponies at one time. A ribby chestnut with a high head carriage and a rolling eye sprang to mind, and a grey with red bandages on its front legs. Clearly I remembered the red bandages. And Richard, sitting easily, elegantly in the saddle, effortlessly in control. Damn Richard, I thought.

Riding lessons had been suggested for me, nat-urally. Riding lessons, swimming, tennis, bell-ring-ing, pottery classes, all had been dangled in front of me at some time in vain effort to persuade me out of the cinema, to prize me away from the television set, to lift my nose out of books on the theatre, out of screen-plays, but all to no avail. Some things I had accepted. Elocution lessons I had attended, ballet dancing, and tap, all three with an eye to their future use, but there had been no room in my life for riding, no use for it at all. Now I wished there had been.

Now, as Miss Evelyn Trubshawe beckoned me and I walked reluctantly across the bark chippings which made for a soft landing towards Pedro and his vacant saddle, I wished with all my heart I had said yes to riding lessons.

7

How Long Does It Take?

Miss Trubshawe took me firmly by the elbow and placed me next to Pedro's shoulder.

'I won't be able to mount,' I told her, 'not possibly. Not without reins and stirrups.'

'Rubbish.' Miss Trubshawe took my left hand and slapped it on to the front of the saddle. 'Bend your left leg from the knee.' Rather reluctantly I raised my left leg and to my alarm felt my ankle taken in a grip of iron. 'On the command of three, spring upwards and throw your right leg over the saddle.'

'I can't,' I protested, 'I won't be able . . .' But on the command of three I found myself being hoisted upwards and somehow my leg went over and I found myself sitting on the saddle. It felt very hard and slippery. I did not like it. Pedro, so fat and solid looking from the ground, looked strangely insubstantial from the saddle. There did not seem to be enough of him to ensure my security. All I could see in front of me was a narrow length of neck topped with ungraspable stubble, ending in two sharp ears. Added to this there was the further inconvenience of having nothing to put my feet in and nothing to hold on to.

'I shan't be able to learn to ride without reins and stirrups,' I said decisively. 'It will be impossible.'

Miss Trubshawe ignored me. Instead she commanded Pedro to 'Walk on!' and Pedro began to circle the enclosure with his jaunty steps, whilst I gripped the front of the saddle, trying desperately not to fall off.

'Relax, Miss Vincent,' trumpeted Miss Trubshawe from the middle of the circle, where she had positioned herself with the lunge rein in one hand and the horrible whip in the other. 'Relax your body completely, and allow your natural balance to assert itself!'

I glowered at her. I felt she should already know that relaxation in such new and alarming circumstances was impossible; that telling me to relax was as unrealistic as an air hostess telling passengers not to worry after informing them that one of the engines had caught fire. I had not taken to Miss Trubshawe on sight, and now I liked her even less. I thought her fat and mean and hideous in her silly black outfit, and I was sure she had deprived me of reins and stirrups out of spite, because she disapproved of me and wanted to make riding appear more difficult than it actually was.

But I only had this single lesson in which to learn to ride, and I had to make the best of it. And so I worked at relaxation, remembering how I had been taught to relax my body at drama school, starting with my jaw, my neck muscles, my shoulders, working downwards through my knee joints, to my ankles, even to my toes. And after a few more circuits I found I was becoming accustomed to the movement of the horse, that there was a rhythm to it, that Pedro's hooves were set down with a soft thud, in a regular sequence, one, two, three, four. And I was able to relax. And because I was able to relax, the movement of the horse was absorbed and followed by my own body. I liked it. I was even able to obey Miss Trubshawe's commands to allow my legs to hang loose and long, and to bring up my chin and look forward between Pedro's sharp little ears, instead of down at the bark chippings.

'Right, Miss Vincent,' Miss Trubshawe boomed, 'let go of the saddle and fold your arms.'

I stared at her. Relaxing was one thing, but letting go of the saddle was quite another.

'Fold your arms, Miss Vincent! You will be quite safe. It will give you confidence to find that you can still balance perfectly well. There is absolutely no necessity to grip the pommel like a drowning man.'

I did not believe it. Cautiously, I let go of the saddle with one hand. I found to my surprise that it was true, I didn't not feel less secure. I loosened my grip with the other hand. Still there was no appreciable lessening of security in the saddle. Finally, I was able to let go of the pommel altogether and I folded my arms.

'Good!' Miss Trubshawe bellowed. 'Now we seem to be getting somewhere!'

I was not sure if this was meant to be a complement or not, but within the next ten minutes my confidence had increased sufficiently to enable me to perform a variety of exercises which included rotating my arms like windmills and touching my toes without altering the position of my legs. Once I had got used to being on a moving animal, I found the exercises easy because I had done similar things at warm-up every morning at the Rose Jefferson Academy and mercifully I was still supple.

After a while, Miss Trubshawe turned Pedro round the circle in the opposite direction and the exercise was repeated. Now I had mastered the exercises and the balance I felt it was time to enquire again about the possibility of having reins and stirrups.

Miss Trubshawe brought Pedro to a halt so swiftly that I almost fell forward on to his neck with my nose in the stubble. 'Miss Vincent, we have been through all this before, and I imagined I had made it clear that you will not be provided with reins or stirrups in this lesson, in the next lesson, or even the one after that.'

It was clear that I would have to explain my situation. 'But there won't be a one after that,' I said, 'or a next lesson. This is the only lesson I can afford, and I need to learn to trot and canter, at least!'

'You mean you were expecting to learn to trot and canter *today*?' Miss Trubshawe's untidily sprouting eyebrows almost vanished into her hairnet. 'In your first *lesson*?'

'It isn't a case of just expecting,' I said. 'I have to do it.'

'Have to do it?' Miss Trubshawe repeated as if she suspected her ears were deceiving her. '*Have* to do it?'

'I have to do it,' I explained, 'because I'm an actress and I've been given a part in a television serial and I'm supposed to be able to ride.'

'But you will never learn to ride in one lesson, Miss Vincent,' Miss Trubshawe said in a scandalized voice. 'You aren't even at the stage when you are ready to trot, heaven only knows when you will be ready for the canter!'

This was exasperating, especially as in my own estimation I had been doing very well. 'I might have been,' I said crossly, 'if I had been given reins and stirrups.'

'Reins and stirrups have nothing to do with it,' Miss Trubshawe snapped. 'When you are in full control of your body without them, when you have achieved a deep and secure seat, and can apply each hand and leg independently, then is the time for reins and stirrups and not before!'

Impasse. We glared at each other across the bark chippings. I now decided that I hated Miss Trubshawe. She had not even tried to understand my situation and she was not prepared to move an inch as far as the lesson was concerned.

Unexpectedly, she said, 'If they wanted someone who could ride for this television serial, why didn't they say so?'

'They did say so,' I said.

The unforgiving eyes narrowed. 'So you lied to them?'

There was no point in denial. 'Yes,' I said.

'I see,' said Miss Evelyn Trubshawe in a crisp voice.

She did not see at all. All she saw proved that I was no better than she had first suspected when I had appeared in my pink leg-warmers and stiletto heels. 'My agent gave me enough money for one lesson,' I said. 'He said one lesson was enough for anybody. He told me that riding was a piece of cake, that I should just think of the horse as a furry bicycle.'

Miss Trubshawe digested this in silence. I thought her lips twitched, but then again, I could have been mistaken.

'Miss Trubshawe, I can't come back for any more lessons,' I said, 'I have no money.'

'I suppose not,' Miss Trubshawe said. 'I suppose like most young people who opt for ludicrously insecure professions, you spend most of your time living on Social Security, quite forgetting that you are being supported by taxes taken from people who have settled for sensible jobs.'

Sensible jobs. Proper jobs. I had heard quite enough of this recently. And somehow it was easier to take from my mother who, for all her disapproval, had only my personal interest at heart; it was even easier to take from Richard who, for all his arrogance, could no more be blamed for his comfortable background than Pedro could be blamed for not being as beautiful as the mahogany horse. But I was not going to take any lectures from Miss Evelyn Trubshawe, a complete stranger, who had no right to disapprove of me and what I chose to do with my life because it was none of her business.

'I am paying you eight pounds for this lesson,' I told her furiously, 'and I am not paying you to lecture me about my career! I am paying you to teach me to ride, and when I say I want to learn to trot and canter, I *mean* it!'

Miss Trubshawe took this rather well. 'All right,' she said in an amenable tone, 'if you feel you must, I suppose we had better get on with it.' Lifting the end of the whip so that it pointed at Pedro's tail, she commanded, 'Pedro, Tr-o-o-t!'

Pedro did trot. Pedro jumped into a trot so quickly that I almost fell off backwards over his rump. Suddenly I found myself banging up and down in the saddle, lurching uncontrollably from side to side, bumping and shaking in the most uncomfortable and alarming manner, and despite Miss Trubshawe's bellowed commands to relax my legs and keep them hanging loose and long, I felt them stiffening and creeping inexorably up the saddle flaps, and despite the fact that I was clinging to the pommel for all I was worth, I felt my whole body slipping dangerously to one side, and the next minute I was sprawled on the bark chippings that made for a soft landing, with all the breath knocked out of my body.

Pedro, who had continued to trot on his accustomed circle, came to an abrupt halt in front of me. He looked at me with interest tinged with alarm, as if uncertain as to how I came to be there. He pointed his ears towards my recumbent form, and snorted a little through his nostrils.

'If you would care to remount, Miss Vincent, we will try to canter next,' Miss Trubshawe said in a level tone.

I managed to get on to my feet. I felt thoroughly shaken and shockingly near to tears. It took Herculean self-control to make nothing of it. 'You did that on purpose,' I said.

Miss Trubshawe neither admitted nor denied it.

'I could have been *injured*,' I said. 'I could have broken an arm or a leg! Even a broken finger would have lost me the part!'

Miss Trubshawe sighed. 'Miss Vincent, I fear you will probably break some part of your anatomy if you are not properly taught,' she said.

I brushed bark chippings off my pink and beige jersey. I took some very deep breaths but still I was shaking so much I was forced to lean against Pedro's shoulder for support. 'Miss Trubshawe,' I gasped in despair, 'how many lessons do I need? How long does it take to learn to ride?'

Miss Trubshawe looked at me thoughtfully, pondering the question as if she had never really considered it before. 'Six months,' she said eventually, 'six years. Sixty years.'

I thought this ridiculous. 'Now wait a minute,' I said. 'I only want to master the basics, I don't want to ride in the Olympics!'

'After twelve lessons you might be able to stay in the saddle,' she said. 'After twenty, you might just be able to pass as a rider.'

'Twelve lessons!' I exclaimed. '*Twenty*!' I thought of Ziggy saying, 'There's nothing to it. You got something to put your feet in, you got leather reins to hold on to, and away you go.' Well, now I knew the truth, and the truth was twelve lessons at a total cost of ninety-six pounds, and that just to enable me to stay in the saddle! With hateful and heartbreaking certainty, I saw the television part slip out of my grasp, and knew that with it I would lose my Equity membership and any hope of work before my year of residence was up at Henry Irving House. 'There is no way I can afford even twelve lessons,' I said.

There seemed no point in getting back into the saddle. Miss Trubshawe coiled up the lungeing rein and led Pedro back to the yard. I followed a little way behind, watching the steel shoes nailed to each of Pedro's hooves as they rose and fell, the way his tail swung from side to side as he walked, noticing the way the white hairs turned to yellow towards the end of the tail, like a smoker's moustache.

In the tackroom I unbuckled the awful hat, pulled off the boots, and sat on the tin trunk to put on my leg-warmers. Miss Trubshawe watched me. Her eyes were not unforgiving any more, they were filled with exasperation.

'You really are going to lose this part, are you, if you can't ride?' she said.

I thought I had already made that perfectly clear. 'It's as good as lost,' I said. And a fat lot you care, I thought, you and your no reins and stirrups nonsense and sixty years to make a rider. I could not bear the thought of having to go back to the Casting Director to confess that I had lied to him, but I knew I would have to do it. Despite Ziggy's optimism, I now knew how difficult riding was, and I also knew it would be impossible to bluff my way through it. Not even *All About Horses and Horse Riding* could help me now.

'And it means a lot to you, this part?'

'Yes.' Keeping my teeth jammed together, I pulled up my leg-warmer and stuck a stiletto on my foot. I could not risk looking up. I did not want Miss Trubshawe to see exactly how much it meant.

'I see.'

I wondered why she persisted in saying 'I see', when it was patently obvious that she did not see at all. In my imagination I saw again the aghast expression on the Casting Director's face when he

69

had said, 'You must be able to ride, Grace Darling! Jesus Christ Superstar, it was *the* audition requirement, we did *say*!' I felt my eyes growing perilously hot.

'At weekends and in the evenings we do get extremely busy here,' Miss Trubshawe said. 'If we need extra help, we usually take schoolgirls to help with the menial tasks.'

I pulled on the second leg-warmer, wishing she would go away. The last thing I wanted was to listen to other people's problems when my own world was about to fall apart.

'It doesn't require any particular skill, but it's hard work, and dirty; mucking out the stables, sweeping the yard, cleaning tack.'

I pushed my feet into my stilettos and stood up. Miss Trubshawe's bulk was still planted squarely in front of me, blocking my escape.

'But if you clock up six hours work,' Miss Trubshawe continued in a relentless voice, 'you do get one hour of tuition free of charge.'

I stared. I wondered if I could have heard correctly. 'You mean you don't take any payment?' I said.

'Free of charge usually means that you don't take any payment,' she said in a testy voice, 'although in this case you would be paying in hard labour.'

I sat down again, somewhat abruptly, on the tin trunk. I looked up at Miss Trubshawe. 'Are you saying you might be prepared to take *me*?' I asked.

'Why shouldn't I take you? Are you averse to hard work, Miss Vincent?'

'No,' I said. 'No, of course not. But I thought

70

you disapproved of me! You told me I was living off taxes paid by people who had sensible jobs!'

'So you are, and I'm entitled to my opinion. But I also think you're in a bit of a spot, and if I can help out, and provided you don't mind a bit of slave labour,' Miss Trubshawe said, 'I think we might have found a way to keep you out of the dole queue – for a little while, at least!'

8

You, Me, and Marcia Cunningham

The film test loomed. Despite Ziggy's assurances that it was just a formality, it assumed monumental importance. It lay ahead, immovable, impenetrable. I could see neither round it nor over it, and it was impossible to imagine what life would be like on the other side of it. The film test barred the way to my future; it was an obstacle I would either negotiate or fail to negotiate, but either way I could not see beyond it.

I wanted to be ready. Everything had to be tidily arranged. In every possible way I felt I had to be prepared. And so, with a deep sense of destiny, akin to that of a dying man, I began to set my affairs in order. I took all my dirty washing to the launderette.

I sorted my clean, but crumpled, clothes. I rolled each item of dancewear and stowed it in my drawstring bag. I zipped my fencing gear into its unwieldy canvas carrying case with my foil and visor. I folded my everyday clothes and put them into my holdall. My forty-three text books (*Voice and the Actor*, *The Actor and his Body*, *A Concise History of the Theatre*, and endless titles by Stanislavsky, Wesker, Brecht, all of them required reading for drama students) I stacked into portable piles and tied each with string. They sat in the middle of the floor, like effects of the deceased, forlornly awaiting my fate.

I cleaned out my room from corner to corner. As a last resort I scrubbed the inside of my cosmetic bag clean of lipstick and mascara smears. I had no way of knowing whether I should depart from Henry Irving in glory or ignominy, but neither would find me unprepared.

On the evening before the film test, when there was no longer anything left to prepare, I sat on my tidy bed in my tidy room, and thought about Richard.

Richard was not tidy. I had said unfair and wounding things to him and now there was bad feeling between us. It did not feel right. It seemed to me that I had done the right thing in the wrong way, that if I had to do the sensible thing and end it, then I should have made it a clean break. Regret would have been in keeping. Sorrow would have been permissible in the face of such finality. But not this untidy parting with frayed ends of hurt, resentment and remorse left dangling. No, I decided, it could not be left like this, I could not afford to leave anything unresolved. If everything was to be tidy, then that included Richard. I wanted all the signs to be prophetic. I got up from my tidy bed, took some coins from my purse, and went downstairs to the pay-phone.

Mercifully, Henry Irving was deserted. Mickey was away on a three-day assignment for a mail-order catalogue, Emma was at her singing lesson. The fencing partners were at rehearsals. It was Lancelot's evening for late-night shopping; I had seen him leave Henry Irving earlier hung with shoulder bags, wearing a jump-suit striped in a zebra

73

pattern accessorized by a brass ear hoop the size of a curtain ring.

When I picked up the receiver my courage almost failed me. Perhaps Richard would refuse to speak to me. Perhaps he would pretend to be out. I looked at my watch. Seven forty-five. Perhaps he *was* out – with Marcia Cunningham. I dialled his home number.

'Wallingford 273.' Richard's voice.

I forced a ten pence piece into the slot. Suddenly my fingers hardly seemed strong enough.

'Richard, it's me, Grace.'

A silence. Then, 'Grace, this is an honour.' The tone was icily polite.

It was difficult to know how to begin. After all, I was not wanting to resume the relationship. I had not telephoned in order to beg. I wanted only to apologize. It ought to be easy.

'I suppose you are ringing to tell me you've landed a starring role?'

The sarcasm rankled.

I had intended to launch straight into apology, but – 'Actually, I have,' I said. 'Actually, I've been chosen to play the female lead in a new Tom Sylvester television serial. I felt I had to ring you with the news. I knew how pleased you would be.'

Two could be sarcastic.

'How very nice for you.' Richard's voice was frosty. In case I imagined that he considered I had achieved anything remotely commendable, he added in a biting tone, 'After all this time.'

I felt myself becoming hot. This was not what I had intended at all. I had not telephoned in order to score points. I just wanted to leave things tidy. 'Richard,' I said, 'you know me. Sometimes I'm hasty. Often I speak before I think. On top of that, I've never found it easy to apologize.'

Richard was not about to make it easier. There was another, more prolonged, silence.

'But now I want to apologize for what I said to you the other day. It wasn't fair. Not only that, it wasn't true.'

'But it showed how you felt nevertheless. And you probably did me a favour in the long run because at least I now know exactly where I stand. I had not realized,' Richard Egan said in a cold voice, 'how much you despised me.'

'Oh Richard, I *don't* despise you,' I said. 'You must know that I don't. How could I? I just hit out at you because you happened to ring when I was having a bad time; I'd had a terrible weekend at home, full of fights and recriminations, and the television part was very much in the balance. I was anxious and frustrated and the people I cared most about seemed to be against me at a time when I badly needed their support – surely you can see that?'

There was a further silence whilst Richard considered this. 'Yes,' he said finally and, it seemed, reluctantly. 'Yes, I can see that.'

The pips went. Heartened, I forced another ten pence piece into Henry Irving's pay-phone. In an effort to lighten the atmosphere I said, 'I have to learn to ride for this part. There's a horse in the story.'

'A *horse*?'

'I'm afraid so. I play a girl who falls in love with a horse she sees in her dreams and then finds him in real life.'

'Hrmmm.' Richard sounded less than impressed.

'I realize it sounds a bit extreme, but it won't be. Not the way Tom Sylvester will write it. He's absolutely brilliant.'

'He sounds as if he needs to be. You seem to have a lot of faith in Tom Sylvester.'

'In this business you need to have faith. Sometimes it's all you *have* got.' Ziggy's words.

'So where are you going to learn to ride?'

'At a stables near Hyde Park. I can't afford to pay for lessons because they're very expensive, but they've said I can work in the yard in exchange for rides.'

'Won't the television company pay?'

'Er . . . the fact is, they don't actually know I can't ride.'

'You mean you bluffed your way into it?'

'You could say that.'

'Well, well,' Richard said in a thoughtful tone as if he must now re-evaluate me as a person capable of such deception. 'You know, I've often thought I should take up riding again. You may not remember, but in my youth I was the leading light of the Wallingford Branch of the Pony Club.'

Typical. 'But you would have been, wouldn't you.' The retort was on my lips before I realized it. 'Simply because your father bought you the best and most expensive ponies.'

'Ah,' said Richard in an I-might-have-known-it-couldn't-last manner.

'But then why not?' I reminded myself I had to keep things tidy. 'I suppose a good pony costs as much to keep as an inferior one.'

'But good ponies do not necessarily make good riders,' Richard said in a dry tone, 'as you will soon discover when you are let loose in Hyde Park.'

Had the ice thawed sufficiently for us to part on good terms? I thought it worth a try. 'Richard,' I began, 'about our relationship.'

'After our last telephone conversation I rather doubted we had one,' he said.

'Yes . . . I mean no; you see, that's why I'm ringing . . .' To my annoyance, now the moment was opportune to explain why I had rung, I was reluctant to do so. I did not want to say it. It could not be because I *wanted* to have a relationship with Richard, I had already made my decision about that. As Emma Hall had said, as an aspiring actress I couldn't afford him, and yet . . . 'Oh *Richard*,' I said, 'I can't bear this bad feeling between us. Please can't we be friends?'

'What kind of friends, Grace?'

'Well,' I said in an uncertain tone, not having really considered it, 'just ordinary, common-or-garden sort of friends . . . Nothing special . . . You know – like you and Marcia Cunningham.'

'I think we'll keep Marcia Cunningham out of this,' Richard decided.

'Quite,' I agreed.

'Are you suggesting, Grace, that you and I should be just casual acquaintances, that sort of thing?' he wanted to know.

'Yes,' I said, relieved to have it said at last,

grateful that he had understood despite the appallingly inept way I had explained it. 'That's *exactly* what I mean.'

'No,' said Richard Egan flatly.

'I'm sorry?' I wondered if I had misheard.

'I said no, Grace. No. No, No, NO!'

We seemed to have covered this ground somewhere before. 'You mean you won't stay friends with me?' I said, astonished.

'Certainly not.'

'You mean you won't speak to me, you'll ignore me, you'll drive past me in the street without even a wave? You can't be serious!'

'I'm deadly serious,' he confirmed. 'If we can't be close friends, then I'm not prepared to be friends at all.'

'*Close* friends?' I said.

'*Close* friends,' he emphasized.

Of course this was typical of Richard. If he couldn't be top dog he wouldn't play. He was spoiled. He always got what he wanted. I knew I should be firm. I knew I should do the right thing in the right way, point out that there would be no hard feelings on my side, that I would always be cordially disposed even if he was not.

'How close is close?' I wondered.

'*Very* close,' he said.

I tried not to imagine the closeness of it. The fair hair falling over the smoothly handsome face, the beautiful, thick-lashed blue eyes looking deeply into mine.

'I have to go for a film test tomorrow,' I told him, 'but after that . . . if you like . . . I mean, only if you wanted me to . . . I *could* come home for a couple of days.'

'*Could* you?' I thought I detected a trace of amusement in his voice.

'Yes. I thought perhaps we could meet sometime . . . go for a drink or something.' Some spark of rebelliousness made me add, 'you know: you, me, and Marcia Cunningham . . .'

I could almost hear the gritting of the perfectly white teeth. Yet Richard restrained himself. 'When did you plan to travel down?' he enquired in a perfectly level voice.

Again, I had not even thought of it. 'I expect it would be Saturday morning,' I said. 'I should probably catch the 11:15 from Victoria.'

'In that case,' he said in a perfectly charming manner, 'we could probably meet you at the station.'

My heart plummeted. 'We?' I said faintly.

'I thought I might bring your mother,' he said.

9

Film Test

Despite the fact that everything was tidy, despite Ziggy's assurances that the film test was nothing to get cooked about, I got off the bus at Whipps Common feeling sick with fright. Had I known what a crazy nightmare I was about to walk into, I might not have got off the bus at all.

Whipps Common consisted of several acres of mown grass dotted with orderly clumps of trees. It was really more of a park, criss-crossed by tarmac paths, and liberally endowed with notices. NO LITTER. NO TRANSISTOR RADIOS. NO BALL GAMES. DOGS MUST BE KEPT UNDER CONTROL AT ALL TIMES.

Parked near the duck pond, NO BATHING. NO POWER BOATS. NO FISHING., was a motley collection of vehicles. As I approached, the door of a caravan opened and the head of the Casting Director appeared. 'Come in, Grace Darling,' he hailed, 'the boys are just grabbing a coffee before we start.'

The 'boys' comprised Ted, the cameraman, who was grey-haired and wore ancient jeans, beaten-up suede shoes and a cardigan; Norm, the sound technician who, though barely out of his twenties, was almost bald but compromised for this slight of nature by the impossible tightness of his leather

trousers, an extravagant excess of gold rings, med-
allions and bracelets, and the discreet use of eye-
liner; Kevin, a location runner, who was nineteen,
skinny, spotty and gormless; and another character,
dark and lean and draped over a bench seat, who
was introduced as 'the handler'. I had never come
across a handler before and regarded him with
apprehension. He looked moody and impatient,
with brooding, restless eyes, and whatever or whoever he was going to handle I hoped it would not be
me.

I had expected Tom Sylvester to be there and was
made even more uneasy to see that he was not. I
wondered why. After auditioning two hundred and
twenty-seven females, surely he was sufficiently
interested in his final choice to want to be present at
the film test. 'Where's the writer?' I asked. 'Isn't he
going to be here?'

The Casting Director handed me a mug of uncom-
promisingly strong, syrupy coffee. 'Nope. The writer's too busy writing. He's holed up in the country
somewhere, finishing the script.'

'Finishing the script? You mean our script? You
mean is isn't even finished yet?' Anxiety made my
voice sharp.

'It's quite normal to start filming before we've got
a complete script, dear heart,' Norm informed me.
'And we do have an insurance policy of sorts –
writers have to give back their advance if they don't
come up with the goods.'

'But what if he *doesn't* come up with the goods?'
I remembered the hibernation into the anorak, the
firmly closed eyes, the unexpected decision to give

81

me the part without hearing me read, the pirouette at the doors. None of these things indicated a stable, reliable temperament. 'Would we still be paid?'

'Paid?' Ted looked up at me in surprise. 'Are you expecting to be paid? And anyway, why do we need a script? I thought the idea was to make it up as we go along.'

'Of course you'll be paid, Grace Darling,' the Casting Director reassured me. 'You're getting paid as from this minute; you can even put in a claim for the taxi fare.'

'Taxi fare?' I asked. 'What taxi fare? I didn't come by taxi, I came by bus.'

'The Star Arrived by Bus,' Ted said in a reflective tone. 'That's quite a good title for a film.'

'Or a book,' Norm put in, 'it's a better title for a book.'

I was not sure if I could handle this. Somehow, the film crew were not at all how I had expected them to be. I had imagined them tough, brisk, professional. Instead they appeared to be a bunch of amiable crackpots. Were they capable of carrying out a film test? Panic began to fill up my chest. I fought it down. 'Where is the make-up artist?' I said in a strangled voice. 'Has she arrived yet?'

'We don't need a make-up artist today,' the Casting Director said. 'We have to see what you look like without paint.'

'We never do much for outside location shots anyway,' Ted explained. 'Natural light's OK. It's studio lighting that drains the colour out of your face.'

I should have known that. The handler gave me a

thin smile which could have been construed as pitying. I hated him. I averted my eyes. 'Where is the co-star?' I demanded. 'Or isn't he coming either?'

'Now hold on, Grace Darling,' the Casting Director said in a soothing tone, 'we're all present and correct, so let's not get anxious.' He detached the mug from my fingers and put it in the sink. There was general upheaval as 'the boys' recognized the need for action and collected up their equipment which included a hand-held camera, which wore its own little fitted jacket. Kevin slapped a slate clapperboard on the table and began to write on it with chalk. TEST, he wrote with painfully slow deliberation, THE HOOFS OF THE HORSES – TAKE ONE. Immediately my stomach twisted itself into a knot. Don't panic, I said to myself, whatever you do, don't lose control. Force yourself to stay calm. Relax your jaw, your neck, your shoulders. Take some slow, deep breaths. None of the self-addressed instructions helped at all.

I followed the crew out of the caravan. I was stiff with fright. I moved like a robot. I knew I would not be able to act to save my life. I would have given anything to have had Ziggy's abrasive, optimistic presence at my elbow. Instead I had Kevin. Outside the caravan he held his clapperboard at arm's length and frowned at it. 'Should it be 'oofs,' he wanted to know, 'or is it 'ooves?' I hadn't a clue.

The Casting Director, still in his shirt-sleeves although there was a chill wind blowing across the common, took charge and began to issue instructions. 'As we're taping the sound last,' he said to

Norm, 'you can drive.' He tossed him a bunch of keys.

'What is he going to drive?' I asked Kevin nervously. 'Are we going somewhere?'

Kevin snapped his clapperboard in an experimental manner. 'We're doing tracking shots,' he informed me, 'didn't you know?'

I did not know. Nor was I certain I knew what tracking shots were. I would have asked for more information, but before I could find the words we were all diverted by the arrival of a man on a bicycle. The man wore a blue uniform with a red stripe down the leg and his peaked cap bore the legend PARK WARDEN. He wobbled towards us looking agitated, waving an arm to gain our attention.

'Jesus Christ Superstar,' the Casting Director muttered, 'what does he want?'

The Park Warden applied his brakes and came to a perilously abrupt halt in front of us. 'You can *read*, I suppose,' he said in an outraged voice. 'You can understand what the sign says? Because it's quite easy to understand, it's perfectly plain. *No* cars on this common, it says, *no* cars, *no* caravans and *no* parking, and that means *everybody*.'

'Now does it really,' Ted said in an interested voice. He lifted his camera on to his shoulder, trained it at the Park Warden, and squinted at him through the lens. 'Because *we* thought it didn't apply to us, didn't we, Norm?'

The Park Warden stiffened. He tried to ignore the attentions of the camera. He was rather too tall for his uniform which looked as though it had been tailored for someone else. His ankles stuck out from the trousers and his knobbly wrists were exposed by the sleeves. He had a long, aggrieved face and a clipped moustache. He took in Norm's exotic appearance and narrowed his eyes. He dismounted from his bicycle and leaned it with deliberate care against a convenient tree. It was new, and furnished with both bell and hooter.

'Do us a favour, sweetheart,' Norm said in an agreeable tone, 'get lost for a bit. By the time you've watered your geraniums and counted your ducks we'll be out of your hair. This is only going to take half an hour.' It was an affable request, but clearly the wrong approach.

The Park Warden glared at him, incensed. 'Get lost? Get *lost!* Who d'you think you're telling to get lost? If anybody's going to get lost, it's going to be you! *You're* the one who's breaking the rules!'

Ted moved in as if to get a closer shot. 'I don't think we'll be going anywhere,' he said. 'We don't care a lot for rules, Norm and me. We find rules a bit of a nuisance really; you know, a bit authoritarian, a bit arbitary . . . most of the time.'

The Park Warden did his best to move out of range. 'Don't you try and get smart with me! Don't get clever!' He stuck out his chin in a challenging manner, 'And don't think I haven't twigged your little game, because I have! It's *pornography*, isn't it!'

Ted lowered his camera and looked at him in genuine amazement. 'Pornography?' he said in an astonished voice. 'At ten o'clock in the morning on a public recreation ground?'

Displaying the pained surprise of a nursery school teacher Norm said, 'My word, what a nasty suspicious mind you have, Mr Park Warden. Go and wash your mouth out with soap.'

'Now hold on a minute,' the Casting Director interceded in a conciliatory tone, 'I'm sure we've all got our jobs to do and it isn't going to help any of us if we get into a slanging match. All I'm asking,' he said in a reasonable voice, placing a hand on the Park Warden's shoulder in a let's-talk-this-over-sensibly-man-to-man sort of way, 'is that you turn a blind eye for twenty minutes so that we can get something in the can. We've got an important television job on here, and I'm sure you're a reasonable man . . .' With his free hand he reached into his back trouser pocket and produced a bulging wallet.

The magic word 'television' acted as an instant palliative and the wallet reinforced the Park Keeper's interest, although he tried hard not to notice it. 'How do I know you'll be finished in twenty minutes,' he said suspiciously.

'You know we'll be finished because we've just told you we will,' Ted assured him. 'It isn't as if we've got much to do. It won't take us long to cut down a couple of trees, light a bonfire . . .'

'. . . roast a pair of mallard, put the washing to dry on the bushes,' added Norm.

The Casting Director pulled a ten pound note out of his wallet. 'Don't take any notice of those two,' he said hastily, 'they've got a crazy sense of humour.'

Kevin chose this moment to snap his clapperboard out of boredom. The Park Warden whipped round as if he had been shot. 'Any more of that, laddie, and I'll have you,' he said in threatening voice.

'Have me for what?' Kevin said in a derisory tone. 'I don't need a licence for this, you know!'

The Casting Director might still have won the day had not the handler, who had been growing more and more impatient by the second, decided to go about his own business, regardless of whether the film crew were with him or not. He began to heave at the side of a lorry parked beside the caravan. The side of the lorry swung smoothly down to meet the grass and became a ramp. At the top of the ramp, looking down at us from behind a partition, was a large black horse.

10
He *Is* the Co-Star . . .

All this was like a terrible nightmare in which the horse was the *piece de resistance*. At the sight of it I wished I could collapse and die on the spot, but it had quite the reverse effect on the Park Warden. He was galvanized into immediate and apoplectic action. He went beserk.

'Oh no you flippin' well don't,' he yelped. 'There's no horse riding allowed on this common, it's in the statutory laws!' He hopped over to the ramp in a red-hot fury and heaved up the end of it. The ramp closed with a resounding thunk, shutting both the handler and the black horse inside.

The Casting Director clutched his temples in despair. 'What did the steaming idiot have to show him the horse for!' Then, turning to the Park Warden: 'I've got to have the horse in the shots,' he insisted in an agonized voice, 'it's mandatory!'

'And I'm telling you, if you fetch that horse out of that lorry, if that animal sets foot on this grass, I'll call the police,' the Park Warden yelled. 'There's no horses allowed on this common except by special permission!'

'I've got special permission,' the Casting Director said.

The Park Warden froze. 'You've got what?'

'I said I've got special permission,' the Casting Director repeated. 'I've got special permission to film that horse on this common. It's signed by the Borough Parks Superintendant himself.'

There was a deep silence around the collection of vehicles whilst everyone evaluated the truth of this statement. The Park Warden stared at the Casting Director in open disbelief. It was clear that he thought it unlikely that such permission had been granted, but he could not afford to ignore the possibility that it might have been. From his position beside the horse box as self-appointed custodian of its contents he said balefully, 'If you'd been given special permission to film horses on my common I'd have been told about it. Nobody's said anything to *me* about special permission.'

'Well, they've probably forgotten to tell you, dear, haven't they?' Norm suggested. 'I wish you'd do as you are told and get lost for a bit. We haven't got all day, you know.'

At this point, the efforts of the handler to lower the ramp from inside the horse box had some effect and the ramp bounced down a little way on its springs, rendering the Park Warden a glancing blow on the top of his peaked cap. Everyone tried hard to keep their faces straight, but Kevin was quite unable to control himself and let out a hoot of delight swiftly arrested by a well aimed kick on the shin administered by one of Ted's beaten-up suede shoes.

The Park Warden, having repositioned himself out of range of the ramp, now produced his trump card. 'If you've got special permission to film horses on this common,' he said triumphantly, 'I want to see it!'

'Well you can't,' the Casting Director told him, 'because I haven't got it. All special permissions are kept in the studio office. I don't carry the paperwork on my person – I'm a film director, not a filing cabinet.'

'And I'm in charge of this common,' the Park Warden declared, 'and what I say is, no special permission in writing, *no* horses, *no* parking, and *no* filming!'

It was an impossible situation, but so far it had been to my advantage because no horse-riding on the common meant that my lack of skill in the saddle would be undetected. Now I felt we were back where we had started, and was even about to suggest that I was filmed speeding along mounted on the Park Warden's bicycle, but to my consternation the Casting Director, who had hitherto been the most patient and reasonable of men, abruptly decided that he had wasted enough time in fruitless negotiation and that Park Warden or no Park Warden, he was going to shoot his film. With increasing dismay I watched as he thrust his wallet back into his trouser pocket, turned to the film crew and began to rap out instructions.

'Kevin, wipe that grin off your face and get the side of that wagon down before they suffocate in there! Ted, make sure there's some film on the reel and get yourself and your camera in the truck! Norm, fit your neat little backside into the driving seat and get the engine running!'

'Oh no you don't!' the Park Warden shouted. 'Not without me seeing your special permission you don't!'

'And who's going to stop me?' the Casting Director enquired heavily. 'Because it isn't going to be you, and that's a fact.'

'Right,' the Park Warden said in a strangled voice. 'Right! You've done it now, mate! Just you wait!' He made for his bicycle.

The pace of the nightmare accelerated. In no time at all the black horse was out of the horse box having its saddle put on by the handler, Norm was in the truck revving at the engine, Ted was arranging himself and his camera half-in, half-out of the passenger seat window. Kevin stood by with his clapperboard.

'OK, Grace Darling,' the Casting Director said, 'let's get you on board.' He gripped my elbow and steered me towards the black horse.

I could not go through with it. I knew there was no way I could pass as a rider. 'Look,' I said desperately, 'I'm not ready for this. I'm upset. I'm not prepared. I haven't brought any riding clothes with me. I can't ride without protective headgear, it's too dangerous. I should have a stand-in for this. Where is the co-star? Let the co-star do it!'

The Casting Director looked at me in amazement. 'What d'you mean, let the co-star do it?' he said. 'The *horse* is the co-star!' His grip on my elbow tightened.

The Park Warden flashed in front of us on his bicycle. His long legs plied the pedals for all he was worth. His face was quite scarlet. 'I'll soon see about special permission!' he shouted at us passionately. 'I'll soon have this sorted! And if I find you're not legitimate when I get through to the Borough Parks

Department, I'll be back! Oh *boy*, will I be back!'
He shot off at an abrupt tangent down one of
the tarmac paths beside which there was a notice
proclaiming NO CYCLING ALLOWED.

Catastrophe was just around the corner and there
was not a thing I could do to prevent it. I was
helpless. The Casting Director propelled me towards
the vacant saddle with steamroller determination
born of many similar situations. There was no possibility of escape, or even argument. 'Listen to me,
Grace Darling,' he said severely, 'there's no time
for you to play temperamental because you know
and I know there's no special permission been
granted, and when that officious little creep finds
out there's going to be all hell let loose.'

The handler grabbed my unwilling ankle and
threw me up on to the saddle in a contemptuous
cavalier manner. I wondered if I should pretend to
faint, but the ground looked too far away. The black
horse was big. Much, much bigger than Pedro. His
neck stretched endlessly in front of me, his black
coat shone like satin, his long mane was slippery,
like silk. He was very, very beautiful, but I knew he
would be the death of me.

I grabbed at the reins. The handler forced my
feet into the stirrup irons. He looked at me suspiciously. 'I hope you've been properly taught,' he
said in an unfriendly voice, 'because I don't allow
my horses to be messed about by novices.'

'You bet she's been properly taught,' the Casting
Director clapped him on his shoulder. 'Grace Darling's just got nerves, that's all.' He turned his
attention toward the camera crew. 'Get that bus on

the pavement, Norm!' he yelled. 'Grace Darling'll track the edge of the grass so you can get the camera an easy ride! Kevin, get the board in the frame then leg it in front and clear the way, we can't afford to kill any of the populace!'

I sat on the black horse with the unfamiliar reins in my hands trying desperately to remember all I had learned from *All About Horses and Horse Riding*. The handler watched me with his hateful dark, suspicious eyes. He said, 'I don't believe you can ride at all, I think you're bluffing.' I loathed him.

Loathing him helped a bit. It gave me back enough courage to try. *'Turn the horse's head towards the direction you wish to take,'* All about Horses and Horse Riding had said, *'Then apply enough pressure with both legs to achieve forward movement.'* In print it had sounded simple. I tried it. With the left rein I turned the black horse's beautiful head in the direction of the truck which was now waiting on the pavement. I squeezed with both legs. To my immense relief, the black horse stepped obediently forward. The handler followed alongside. 'If you can't ride, you had better say so now,' he said, 'otherwise I won't answer for the consequences.' I ignored him.

I rode the black horse to the truck. Drawing on what I had learned from Miss Evelyn Trubshawe, I told myself to relax, to keep my legs loose and long. I placed myself in the deepest part of the saddle. If I can just stay in control, I thought, if I can just manage to stay in the saddle, I might survive this. I was frightened. I felt weak and hot. My heart was fluttering like a butterfly in a jamjar, but at that point I honestly believed there was a chance I might get away with it.

At the truck I asked the black horse to halt. '*Close the legs on to the horse and push him up into a fixed hand,*' my book had said, '*but on no account should the hands be drawn backwards or exert a direct pull on the horse's mouth.*' When I had read this I had not understood it, nor did it make sense now, but the black horse seemed to understand what was required of him and stopped. I managed to let go of the reins long enough to give him a grateful pat. The handler watched with eyes of steel. He took a whistle on a cord out of his pocket and hung it round his neck.

The Casting Director stood on the pavement holding a loud hailer. 'Now, Grace Darling, I want you to keep to the edge of the grass and stay as near to the camera as you can until I tell you otherwise. Ted will tell you what he wants, and I'll warn you what the horse is going to do. There's no need to give any instructions to the beast yourself because he's trained to the whistle.'

This was an unexpected and alarming development. I glanced down at the handler. He gave me a hostile look and placed the whistle between his teeth.

'OK,' the Casting Director said impatiently, 'let's see some action.'

From the truck Ted gave me a reassuring grin. He applied himself to his camera. Kevin jumped in front of the black horse with his clapperboard. The next minute, almost without knowing how I had achieved it, I was riding the black horse along the edge of the common with the truck crawling alongside and Ted's steady voice issuing from behind the camera. 'Look to the front, sweetheart . . . Now to me . . . Smile a bit . . . Say something to me . . . Now look down at the horse . . . Fuss over him a bit . . . tell him something, lean over him, whisper sweet nothings in his ears . . . That's great . . . Stick with it . . .'

'OK, cut the cackle, let's *move*!' the Casting Director bellowed. There was a single, piercing blast on the whistle. The black horse swivelled a silken ear and went forward into a long-striding trot. I told myself to relax, to let my body absorb the movement. The truck accelerated along the pavement. I began to bang about uncontrollably in the saddle. 'Whoa,' I said to the black horse, 'slow down a bit.' He didn't appear to hear me.

'Get your head up, sweetheart!' Ted shouted. 'Look forward! Let your hair blow back in the wind! Now look at me! Laugh at me!'

Laughing was the last thing I felt like. I lost a stirrup. I abandoned the reins and grabbed the front of the saddle. I felt my legs stiffening. My knees were creeping up the saddle flaps.

'OK. Let's speed it up!' roared the Casting Director.

Two blasts on the whistle followed. The black horse leapt forward into a canter. Wind rushed past my face. Hooves thudded on the grass. The black neck stretched ahead and the silken mane flew for the benefit of the camera, but all I could feel was the familiar, horrifying sensation of my whole body slipping to one side, towards the close-cropped, speeding turf, with no bark chippings to make for a softer landing.

The Park Warden delivered the *coup de grâce*. Having discovered that no special permission had been granted to film horse riding on the common, he returned with all possible speed and suddenly shot out on his bicycle from a clump of trees to my left, in order to position himself in an heroic but ill-advised manner exactly in the black horse's path.

The black horse faltered in his stride fractionally, but he was trained to the whistle, and blindly, faithfully obedient to it. An experienced rider might have stopped him, could perhaps have turned him, but I was in no position to impede his progress from half-way down his shoulder where I was clinging, grimly but unsuccessfully, to the slippery, satin neck. Unable to veer either to the left because of the trees, or to the right because of the cruising truck, the brave black horse took the only course of action open to him, gathered himself together, and attempted to jump the obstacles in his path.

He might have succeeded had not the Park Warden, his face frozen into a mask of terror, tried to drag his bicycle out of range in the final seconds before flinging himself clear. But as the black horse soared and I was catapulted on to the grass under the trees, where I landed with a breath-taking, bone-shaking impact, the bicycle moved and, as a result, took the full force of the horse's forehand as it landed in an appalling cacophony of metallic twangings, bucklings, the pinging of spokes, and an agonized honk as the hooter was flattened by a large black hoof. To compound this double disaster the truck, in making a well-intentioned but posthumous swerve out towards the road to allow the black horse room to manoeuvre, had its progress noisily and abruptly arrested when it came into contact with the base of a concrete lamp-post.

In the few seconds that followed one might have imagined that the whole world had come to a halt in silent sympathy. I lay on the ground too shocked and horrified to move. It crossed my mind that my injuries might be so great that I may never move again. Ahead of me, the black horse, with two of its legs imprisoned within the spokes of a bicycle wheel, hopped along the grass for a short distance then, sensibly declining to panic, came to an awkward halt and waited for outside assistance.

Outside assistance was heralded by the sound of running feet as the world came to life. The handler arrived first, pounding past my prone form in a white-hot rage on his way to rescue the black horse. 'Of all the stupid, empty-headed little fools,' he screamed as he flew by, 'I *knew* you couldn't ride the minute I saw you! Have you any idea how much damage you could have done? Have you any idea how much this horse is *worth*?'

The Casting Director came puffing up behind, still clutching his loud-hailer. The Park Warden immediately launched into the attack. 'Fifteen years I rode my old bicycle,' he shrieked, 'fifteen years! Last week they gave me a new one!' He grabbed the Casting Director by the shirt-sleeve and dragged him towards the spot were the handler, with loving, soothing words, was trying to extricate the black horse from the wheels.

In the vicinity of the truck, the camera in its own little jacket lay on the pavement where it had been precipitated at the moment of impact, surrounded by shards of glass from one of the headlights. Ted and Norm were engaged in a private battle. 'You bloody stupid berk!' Ted yelled. 'Don't tell me you didn't notice a bloody great pile of concrete when it was right in front of your sodding nose!'

Nobody seemed to care whether I was alive or dead, but certainly they now knew that I was both a liar and a fraud. Painfully, slowly, I managed to get to my feet. I felt no joy in the realization that I still retained the use of all of my limbs. All I wanted was to get away. As I stumbled across the common, snatches of furious argument followed me.

'Don't talk to me about special permission because *I* know there's none been granted . . .' 'If this horse had broken a leg he would have had to be shot, have you *any* idea . . .' 'Six thousand quid's worth of camera up the spout, and all because a bloomin' idiot can't see the nose in front of his rotten face . . .' And over it all the desperate pleading of the Casting Director, 'Now look, fellas, it's not going to help anybody if we get all het up . . .'

By the first stroke of good fortune to come my way all day, a bus was just about to draw away from the request stop. Putting on a painful spurt to cross the road, I just managed to catch it.

11
Finale

'. . . and then the handler called me a stupid, empty-headed little fool, and everyone started fighting, and so I walked across the common and got on the bus.'

I could not bring myself to look at Ziggy as I related this. Instead, I concentrated upon dislodging a piece of dried spaghetti which had glued itself to one of the tiles on the table-top. Half a day and a sleepless night had passed before I could summon enough courage to face this encounter, and when I had finally forced myself to walk into the Café Marengo it had been a relief to see Ziggy sitting alone in his corner booth. Ironically, an audience was now the last thing in the world I wanted.

Ziggy said nothing. If he had blamed me, if he had set about me with recriminations, I could have coped. I could have cried that it was his fault for sending me to audition without telling me that horse riding ability was the prime requirement. I could have berated him for saying that horse riding was a piece of cake, that one lesson was enough for anybody. But Ziggy said nothing and it was not easy to cope with. Keeping my eyes on the piece of spaghetti, I said, 'I know you think I've thrown away the best part I'm ever likely to be offered. I do understand how you feel, but I want you to know, Zig, how hard I tried. I honestly don't believe that anyone could have tried harder.'

Still there was no response. The piece of spaghetti began to blur in front of my eyes. It was quite appalling how often I had found myself near to tears in the last few days. Not only did it seem that I had lost control of events, but also of my emotions. It was a bad sign. Before this, I had never seriously doubted that I had what it took to make an actress, that I had the necessary grit. Now I was not so confident. Suddenly I began to doubt myself.

None of this would have escaped Ziggy's notice. And by now I knew him well enough to know that not only had I lost the part, I had also lost my agent. Ziggy was not the kind of person who had the time or the patience to nurture a delicate plant or massage a bruised ego. Ziggy wanted no truck with clients who were emotional or temperamental. What he wanted was a fighter, a hard-boiled surviver who could take all the punches, who could take any amount of rejections on the chin, who could be knocked out for the count one minute and be up and fighting again the next. Well, there had been a time when I honestly believed I qualified, but when the opportunity to show my true mettle had come, I had not even lasted the first round.

'Mr Stanislavski!' Mr Vincinelli called. 'Is young lady on my telephone to speak with you!' From behind the counter he waved the receiver urgently.

'I told you I don't speak with young ladies on the telephone,' Ziggy replied, 'especially not now, I'm busy.'

'But this is five times now she ring,' Mr Vincinelli protested. 'This is five times in two days and she is most insisting. And I remember this young lady because she have a very big voice and frighten away my customers!'

Emma Hall. Emma Hall was a tough cookie, I thought. Emma Hall was a fighter who wouldn't let a prize slip through her fingers. She would have been in there punching for the part until the end. Emma Hall would not have crept away across the common and wept silent tears on the back seat of the bus all the way home. I wondered what had happened to me. At the Rose Jefferson Academy where the fall out rate during training had been six out of ten, I had been told that seventy per cent of those who graduated became discouraged and disillusioned and gave up within two years of leaving drama school. Was I about to become one of that seventy per cent? After all I had been through? After weathering the disapproval of family and friends? After three years' hard slog at the Rose Jefferson Academy? After thirty auditions, had the fact that I had been so near to success only to have it snatched from my grasp, finally snapped my spirit?

'Tell Emma Hall to go take a running jump,' Ziggy said. 'Tell her I don't take personal calls, least of all from people who need singing lessons.'

Mr Vincinelli relayed this in a harassed voice, and banged down the receiver. 'She say fine,' he cried in exasperation, 'she say fine, she ring again tomorrow! I tell you Mr Stanislavski, I have many, many things to do instead of answer my telephone! What you try to do to me? You try to ruin my business?'

'I told you what to do,' Ziggy told him. 'Get me a separate line installed. I'll pay the rental.'

'Get him a line installed,' muttered Mr Vincinelli,

'get him a line installed!' In his indignation he addressed a customer sitting in solitary state at the counter. 'Do you hear what he say to me? Get him a line installed! I ask you one simple question; is this his business, or is it mine?' He snatched up the customer's cup and saucer. 'You want more coffee? I give you one for nothing! What do I care!' He vanished behind the espresso machine to vent his annoyance in a welter of angry gurglings, furious boilings and whooshings of steam. The customer turned round on his stool and gave us a look of complete bewilderment.

But the silence at the table in the corner booth of the Café Marengo remained unbroken. I had one more try. 'I know you are angry with me,' I said, 'I know I've lost you money, and I know you won't want to be my agent any more, why should you? But before I go, I just want to say how much I've appreciated your help, and how dreadfully sorry I am that it hasn't worked out.'

Still I could not look at him. If I had lost undreamed of riches with the part, I had not been the only loser. I was to have been paid five hundred pounds a week whilst I was filming, plus a retainer of fifty pounds a week until I received the script, then a hundred pounds a week until filming started. Out of this Ziggy would have taken his ten per cent which, at a time of abnormally high unemployment, when even more than the usual eighty per cent of Equity members were without work, was a substantial sum for an agent to lose.

No wonder Ziggy felt sore. No wonder he got up from the table in disgust. No wonder he slung his leather blouson with the appliquéed silver star over his shoulder and paused for a brief word with Mr Vincinelli, cocking a thumb in my direction to indicate that I was now an ex-client, someone of no account, a no-hoper, a person to be got rid of at the earliest opportunity. No wonder he went out of the Café Marengo without a backward glance, leaving me abandoned in the corner booth.

Of all the rejections I had suffered, this was by far the most wounding. Ziggy had not only been my agent, in his uncompromising way he had been my mentor, my champion and my comfort. He had never told me it would be easy and it had not been. He had never promised me success and there had not been any. He had never offered me his friendship, but I had honestly believed him to be my friend. Now I knew differently.

Had it not been for Mr Vincinelli and the solitary customer at the counter, I might have laid my head on the tile-topped table and howled my eyes out. In the circumstances it would not have been an extreme reaction to my predicament. I had no job, no money apart from unemployment benefit, no agent, and in three weeks I had to move out of Henry Irving House because my year was up. What did I do now? Did I hoof it yet again round the established agencies, hoping that one of them would take pity on me and ask to hear my well-worn audition pieces; the feminist monologue from *Waking Up* by Fo and Rame; the plea of Portia from *The Merchant of Venice*:

> *'You see me, Lord Bassanio, where I stand,*
> *Such as I am. Though for myself alone*

103

I would not be ambitious in my wish
To wish myself much better. Yet for you
I would be trebled twenty times myself –
A thousand times more fair, ten thousand times
More rich.
That only to stand high in your account,
I might in virtues, beauties, livings, friends,
Exceed account . . .'

Of course, there were many jobs open to out-of-work actresses, *The Stage and Television Today* was full of them. I could promote the latest lines in scent and after-shave in Harrods or Harvey Nichols; I could sell life assurance over the telephone; I could conduct market research in the streets; I could even dress up as a serving wench at the Court of King Harry for the benefit of roistering, mead-swilling tourists. But would any of these jobs give me artistic satisfaction? Would they lead to something better if I accepted them? I knew they would not. I knew that the sensible thing to do was to go back to Wallingford, enrol on a secretarial course, acquire marketable skills, and settle down in a 'proper job'. The thought was unbearable.

And what about Richard? Foolishly, out of pique, I had told Richard that the television part was definite, and by now everyone in Wallingford would know of it. Somehow I had to face them, but facing Richard would be the worst. I could imagine his reaction. I remembered the frosty reception to the news that I had landed the part. The wintry manner in which he had said 'How very nice for you.' The biting way he had added '. . . after all this time.' How could I now admit that I had lied? How could

I go back and admit to the whole village that I had lied?

Perhaps I should consider staying on, but how would I afford it, once I had left Henry Irving? In some, grim, down-at-heel area on the periphery of the city I might find a room for less than forty pounds a week, and if I could not persuade another agent to take me on, then I would have to steel myself to do what some of the tougher female graduates from drama schools had historically always done; launch myself upon the seedy, second rate nightclub scene as an 'exotic dancer', just centimetres away from a stripper, for the sole purpose of gaining Equity membership. Could I do it? Well, once I had never thought myself capable of lying my way into a part, but I had done it. Once I would not have dreamed of lying to Richard but I had done that as well. Pride and the fear of failure had turned me into a liar, and now threatened to make me an exotic dancer – what next on the downward path?

Overcome by despair and self-pity, I allowed several teardrops to drip on to the tabletop of the Café Marengo. Instantly a cloth appeared beneath my downturned face and wiped them away. I looked up to see Mr Vincinelli standing beside me. In one hand he clutched the cloth, and in the other, red paper napkins and cutlery. He smiled at me in an uncertain manner, as if an attempt at cheerfulness in the face of such obvious distress might be interpreted as wholly unsympathetic.

Poor, long-suffering Mr Vincinelli had obviously been told to get rid of me, but he could not bring himself to ask me to leave. Instead he began to lay the table as if it had been reserved for a meal, which was unheard of in the Café Marengo. Place mats appeared. Wine glasses. A salt and pepper mill. A glass ashtray. A candle in a Chianti bottle. Menus, painstakingly wiped clean of coffee-rings and specks of bolognese sauce. Mr Vincinelli gave me a hesitant, encouraging pat on the top of my head.

'It's all right,' I managed to say. 'I'm going now.'

Mr Vincinelli drew back in a startled manner. 'Going? You mean you go out of the Café Marengo? But Mr Stanislavski, he say . . .'

'Mr Stanislavski, he say you stay right where you are, Kiddo.' A hand with a familiar thick silver identity bracelet on the wrist thrust a bunch of multi-coloured freesias under my nose. The black leather blouson with the appliqué silver star was tossed on to the opposite bench seat. The blouson was followed by Ziggy himself.

Over the place mats, the wine glasses, the menus, I stared at Ziggy. My mind began to race. Once again my heart began to flutter like a butterfly in a jamjar.

Mr Vincinelli scuttled away to the counter and returned with a bottle of Frascati which, with a great deal of concentrated effort, he managed to open. 'You like to taste the wine, Mr Stanislavski?' he enquired.

'And if I don't care for the taste,' Ziggy wanted to know, 'will the next bottle be any different?'

'I am afraid that it is most possible it will be the same,' apologized Mr Vincinelli. He splashed the wine into the glasses. He smiled fondly at us both.

With his free hand he gave me a further and more confident pat on the top of my head.

I looked at Mr Vincinelli's beaming face. I looked at the freesias. I looked at Ziggy. Ziggy grinned at me across the crowded tabletop. He shrugged his shoulders slightly.

An impossible, incredible thought occurred to me. It could not be true. And yet somehow I knew it was. I could not trust myself to speak. My throat had closed. Tears flooded my eyes and coursed down my cheeks. Mr Vincinelli gave me a paper napkin to utilise as a handkerchief.

Ziggy leaned over the table and picked up the hand still clutching the freesias. He detached them from my fingers. He sent Mr Vincinelli to find a vase. He didn't give my hand back, he kept it, held fast between his own, on his side of the table. 'I got the bell this morning, Kiddo,' he said. 'Never mind the aggro. Forget the horse-riding because they're sending you on a course to learn how to do it. The test came out great. You got the part. They love you, Grace Darling!'

Fiction in paperback from Dragon Books

Peter Glidewell

Schoolgirl Chums	£1.25 ☐
St Ursula's in Danger	£1.25 ☐
Miss Prosser's Passion	£1.50 ☐

Enid Gibson

The Lady at 99	£1.50 ☐

Gerald Frow

Young Sherlock: The Mystery of the Manor House	95p ☐
Young Sherlock: The Adventure at Ferryman's Creek	£1.50 ☐

Frank Richards

Billy Bunter of Greyfriars School	£1.25 ☐
Billy Bunter's Double	£1.25 ☐
Billy Bunter Comes for Christmas	£1.25 ☐
Billy Bunter Does His Best	£1.25 ☐
Billy Bunter's Benefit	£1.50 ☐
Billy Bunter's Postal Order	£1.50 ☐

Dale Carlson
Jenny Dean Mysteries

Mystery of the Shining Children	£1.50 ☐
Mystery of the Hidden Trap	£1.50 ☐
Secret of the Third Eye	£1.50 ☐

Marlene Fanta Shyer

My Brother the Thief	95p ☐

David Rees

The Exeter Blitz	£1.50 ☐

Caroline Akrill

Eventer's Dream	£1.50 ☐
A Hoof in the Door	£1.50 ☐
Ticket to Ride	£1.50 ☐

Michel Parry (ed)

Superheroes	£1.25 ☐

Ulick O'Connor

Irish Tales and Sagas	£2.95 ☐

To order direct from the publisher just tick the titles you want
and fill in the order form.

Fiction in paperback from Dragon Books

Mr T	£1.50	☐
Ann Jungman		
Vlad the Drac	£1.25	☐
Vlad the Drac Returns	£1.25	☐
Vlad the Drac Superstar	£1.50	☐
Jane Holiday		
Gruesome and Bloodsocks	£1.25	☐
Thomas Meehan		
Annie	£1.50	☐
Michael Denton		
Eggbox Brontosaurus	£1.25	☐
Glitter City	£1.25	☐
Fantastic	£1.25	☐
Marika Hanbury Tenison		
The Princess and the Unicorn	£1.25	☐
Alan Davidson		
A Friend Like Annabel	£1.25	☐
Just Like Annabel	£1.25	☐
Maureen Spurgeon		
BMX Bikers	£1.50	☐
BMX Bikers and the Dirt-Track Racers	£1.50	☐
T R Burch		
Ben and Blackbeard	£1.25	☐
Ben on Cole's Hill	£1.25	☐
Jonathan Rumbold		
The Adventures of Niko	£1.25	☐
Marcus Crouch		
The Ivory City	95p	☐
Lynne Reid Banks		
The Indian in the Cupboard	£1.50	☐
Nina Beachcroft		
A Spell of Sleep	£1.25	☐
Cold Christmas	£1.50	☐
Graham Marks		
The Finding of Stoby Binder	£1.50	☐
David Osborn		
Jessica and the Crocodile Knight	£1.50	☐

To order direct from the publisher just tick the titles you want
and fill in the order form.

Fiction in paperback from Dragon Books

Richard Dubleman
The Adventures of Holly Hobbie   £1.25 ☐

Anne Digby
Trebizon series
First Term at Trebizon   £1.50 ☐
Second Term at Trebizon   £1.50 ☐
Summer Term at Trebizon   £1.50 ☐
Boy Trouble at Trebizon   £1.50 ☐
More Trouble at Trebizon   £1.50 ☐
The Tennis Term at Trebizon   £1.50 ☐
Summer Camp at Trebizon   £1.50 ☐
Into the Fourth at Trebizon   £1.25 ☐
The Hockey Term at Trebizon   £1.50 ☐
The Big Swim of the Summer   60p ☐
A Horse Called September   £1.50 ☐
Me, Jill Robinson and the Television Quiz   £1.25 ☐
Me, Jill Robinson and the Seaside Mystery   £1.25 ☐
Me, Jill Robinson and the Christmas Pantomime   £1.25 ☐
Me, Jill Robinson and the School Camp Adventure   £1.25 ☐

Elyne Mitchell
Silver Brumby's Kingdom   85p ☐
Silver Brumbies of the South   95p ☐
Silver Brumby   85p ☐
Silver Brumby's Daughter   85p ☐
Silver Brumby Whirlwind   50p ☐

Mary O'Hara
My Friend Flicka Part One   85p ☐
My Friend Flicka Part Two   60p ☐

To order direct from the publisher just tick the titles you want
and fill in the order form.

All these books are available at your local bookshop or newsagent, or can be ordered direct from the publisher.

To order direct from the publishers just tick the titles you want and fill in the form below.

Name _____

Address _____

_____

Send to:
Dragon Cash Sales
PO Box 11, Falmouth, Cornwall TR10 9EN.

Please enclose remittance to the value of the cover price plus:

UK 45p for the first book, 20p for the second book plus 14p per copy for each additional book ordered to a maximum charge of £1.63.

BFPO and Eire 45p for the first book, 20p for the second book plus 14p per copy for the next 7 books, thereafter 8p per book.

Overseas 75p for the first book and 21p for each additional book.

Dragon Books reserve the right to show new retail prices on covers, which may differ from those previously advertised in the text or elsewhere.